the one who was standing apart

from me

the one who was standing apart

from me

( )

Maurice Blanchot

translated by Lydia Davis

BARRYTOWN
STATION HILL

Published by Station Hill Literary Editions, under the Institute for Publish-
ing Arts, Inc., Barrytown, New York 12507. Station Hill Literary Editions
is supported in part by grants from the National Endowment for the Arts,
a Federal Agency in Washington, D.C., and by the New York State Council
on the Arts. The translation was funded in part by a grant from the New
York State Council on the Arts.

Cover designed by George Quasha and Susan Quasha.

Library of Congress Cataloging-in-Publication Data

Blanchot, Maurice.
     [Celui qui ne m'accompagnait pas. English]
     The one who was standing apart from me / Maurice Blanchot :
     translated by Lydia Davis.
          p. cm.
     ISBN 0-88268-053-6 (cloth) — ISBN 0-88268-151-6 (pbk.)
     I. Title.
PQ2603.L3343C413   1992
843'.912—dc20   92-19395
                                                                   CIP

Manufactured in the United States of America.

the one who was standing apart
_____
from me

I sought, this time, to approach him. I mean I tried to make him understand that, although I was there, still I couldn't go any farther, and that I, in turn, had exhausted my resources. The truth was that for a long time now I had felt I was at the end of my strength.

"But you're not," he pointed out.

About this, I had to admit he was right. For my part, I was not. But the thought that perhaps I did not have "my part" in mind made it a bitter consolation. I tried to put it another way.

"I would like to be." A manner of speaking which he avoided taking seriously; at least, he didn't take it with the seriousness that I wanted to put into it. It probably seemed to him to deserve more than a wish. I continued to reflect on what "I wanted." I had noticed that he was interested in facts, he became more exacting and perhaps more sincere when it was possible to speak to him in the language everyone spoke, and that language certainly seemed to be the language of facts. Yet the obstacle was that—just then— events seemed to have receded extraordinarily. He came to my assistance in his own way.

"It seems to me," I said, "that in a sense I have everything, except..."

"Except?"

I had the impression he was more attentive now, even

though that attention was not directed at me, but was, instead, a silent direction, a hope for himself, a sort of daybreak which, finally, revealed nothing more than the word "except." A little more, nevertheless, for I was induced to add:

"Except that I would like to be rid of it."

I believe that, despite everything, I expected from him an invitation to go forward, and perhaps also a risk, an obstacle. I wasn't fighting, but I wasn't yielding either, yielding would have required more strength than I had. I can't deny that the need to talk to him, and most often to be the first to talk—as though what I had was the initiative, while he had the discretion, the concern to leave me free, though even that might have been only impotence on his part, and consequently impotence on my part too—this need seemed to me so exhausting, so tormenting, that often I didn't even have enough real strength left to make use of it. I didn't have the feeling that talking was in the least necessary to him, or pleasant, or unpleasant either. He always displayed an extreme loyalty; with the greatest firmness he brought me back from a word that was less true to a word that was more true. Sometimes I wondered if he was not trying to restrain me at all costs. I came to believe that he had always barred my way, even though, if he showed any intention, it was, rather, that of helping me to be done with it. According to him—but I must add that he never declared this to me with as much precision as I am doing—I came closest to his help when I made up my mind to write. He had assumed a strange ascendancy over me in all these things, so that I had allowed myself to be persuaded that to write was the best way of making our relations bearable. I admit that for some time this way was quite good. But one day I noticed that what I was writing concerned him more and more and, though in an indirect manner, seemed to have no other purpose but to reflect him. I was extremely struck by this discovery. In it I saw what might paralyze me the most, not because I would

2

henceforth try to avoid this reflection, but because, on the contrary, I might go to more trouble to make it manifest. It was then that I caught hold of myself. I knew—but I did not exactly know it, I hoped—that the need to say "I" would allow me to have better mastery over my relations with this reflection. I think personal honesty, personal truth, seemed to me to have something specific about them, capable of momentarily giving me the security of a point of view. Nevertheless, the consequences for my life were disastrous. Not only did I have to give up what is called a normal life, but I lost control of my choices. I also became afraid of words and I wrote fewer and fewer of them, even though the pressure exerted inside myself to make me write them soon became dizzying. I speak of fear, but it was a completely different feeling, a sort of erosion of the future, the impression that I had already said more about it than was possible for me, that I had gotten ahead of myself in such a way that the possibility farthest in the future was already there, a future I could no longer go beyond. At the same time, I forced myself into the fiction of a legal life. I don't know if such a concern wasn't a mistake. My intention was to do nothing that could surprise and interest the world to the extent that it was aware of my conduct and my way of being. This compelled me into all sorts of subterfuges and even a general lie on which, I fear, much of my strength was spent and which, in turn, incited me to stiffen myself excessively against the most innocent activities. In addition to these difficulties, which I am rapidly passing over, there was another, and that was that they did not help me in any way to settle my relations with him, relations in view of which, nevertheless—and thinking, perhaps at his suggestion, that writing was the place where I could be the least bothered by his presence—I had little by little put myself in an almost intolerable situation.

In truth, it was possible that for some time he had been giving me considerable help. He had put me to my task by creating a void around that task and probably by letting me believe that the task would be able to limit and circumscribe the void. This was really how it was, in fact, at least apparently, and even though during the same time I had to go through events so terrible that it would be better to say they went through me and they are still, ceaselessly, going through me, I enjoyed a strange illusion that allowed me not to see that already I should no longer be speaking of task, but of life. This illusion represented a diversion, but also a power that I had acquired for myself. Unconcern was the only gift by which I was capable of drawing it with me into the broad daylight. A moment's success, but in no way diminished by that, since success consisted precisely in joining life and moment. Once the moment was past, the unconcern died away, but the face it had illuminated did not die away, or its manner of darkening was that darkness also became its face. There too, it is possible that he helped me by turning me away from responsibility for the world, by wrapping me in an ambiguous silence that depended as much on my refusal to converse with him as on the fact that in truth, without realizing it, I spoke to him constantly through this very refusal. A help which, if it occurred, consisted in turning my attention away from an event, and an image, with which I could never have behaved in a way that was natural and real, reserved and discreet, without a state of half-attention and almost of indifference. But if writing turned me into a shadow to make me worthy of the darkness, I must certainly also think that this maneuver succeeded more than it should have, for I pushed reserve and discretion so far, from this point of view, that not only did I do nothing to trouble those moments, but they did not trouble me either, so that my memory of them makes me wander tragically in the void. All this, all these events, which are so difficult to recapture and grow indistinct through their own presence, all these difficulties, these demands, these efforts, and now this immobility, from which my desire has more and more trouble preserving me, this situation, which is so strange but has be-

4

come so familiar to me that I can almost no longer refuse to understand it—was all this destined to result in that one sentence: "I sought, this time, to approach him"? "This time," I saw clearly how unjustified such a remark seemed. It appeared there because I wanted to be at the end of my strength. But for my part, I was not, and for such a part "this time" was not "this time," but another time, a time that was always another. I can't hide the fact that the desire to approach him could only with great difficulty be reconciled with the idea that this could ever take place "this time." He did nothing to ward off such an event. It may even be that he awaited it with a sort of hope. But I felt that the whole enterprise was entrusted to me alone, and I must say I wasn't managing it, I wasn't managing it.

"You get by well enough," he remarked. "You're astonishing, you know."

Yes, I got by quite well, but this in itself cast a not very engaging light on everything I could imagine doing; I got by all too well, whereas the best that could have happened to me would have been not to get by at all.

He did not fail to encourage me, but in his own way, and that way was strange, discouraging, for it consisted in assuring me that I had all the time in the world. No doubt the sort of decision inaugurated by my desperate and arbitrary recourse to "this time" implied that until now I had never yet approached him in a spirit of preoccupation, intention, not to say inquisition. I retained the memory of not having done so, not out of fear, but because "I didn't have the time" and simply because I didn't concern myself about it. If I now had all the time in the world, it was therefore because I had given up all other interests but him and in fact all interests, for— and this was the ludicrous aspect of the situation—I couldn't interest myself in him, I could only accord him this lack of interest, this sadness of my inattention that made every presence sterile. He accommodated himself to this, of course, but he seemed to doubt it also, even though in expressing his doubt he never went farther than this phrase:

"Oh, it's not such a necessary thing!"

And what he meant by that had this rather edifying sense:

"Oh, I am not so interested in myself!"

It's true that I could derive another, more convincing inference from his mysterious words of encouragement, that on the whole I didn't have to be afraid of the false steps, the itineraries of error; I didn't have just one road, I had them all, and this should, in fact, have encouraged me to start on my way with an exceptional confidence.

"All of them! But on condition that I have all the time in the world, as long as I have all the time in the world."

He didn't deny it, for it was clearly understood that the characteristic of a road was to provide a shortcut through "time"; it was this shortcut I was looking for, with the unreasonable idea that in it I would find, not what would still be a very long tramp, but the shortest interval, the essence of brevity, to the point that, from the first steps, it seemed to me, refusing to go farther, that I had the right to say to myself: "I'm staying here," and that was what I said to him with greater firmness: "I'm staying here, I'm stopping here," to which he happened precisely to respond with a sort of enthusiasm and without my being able to take it the wrong way: "But you have all the time in the world."

From him, I couldn't take anything the wrong way. I didn't know where or how all this was going to end. He had become my travelling companion, but I couldn't assert that we had everything in common, or else that community would have signified that he had everything in common with me and I nothing with him, if we had not clearly tended to have nothing, either one of us. I couldn't attribute bad intentions to him, for he was extraordinarily lacking in intentions. I supposed he was helping me, but I should say his help was such that it left me, more than anything else, at a loss, unfit, and indifferent to being helped in any way, and only a sort of obstinacy permitted me to think that this assistance could be called help and even the greatest possible help. True, I did not always recognize this. I had noted with surprise, with a slight feeling of strangeness, but eventually with discomfort and without surprise, that he was probably lacking enough in intentions to deflect my own, to lead them to the point where they would have to identify with this deflection. I could recall, as an intoxicating navigation, the motion that had more than once driven me toward a goal, toward a land that I did not know and was not trying to reach, and I did not complain that in the end there was neither land nor goal, because, in the meantime, by this very motion, I had lost my memory of the land, I had lost it, but I had also gained the possibility of going forward at random, even though, in fact, consigned to this randomness, I had to renounce the hope of ever stopping. The consolation could have been to say to myself: You have renounced foreseeing, not the unforeseeable. But the consolation turned around like a barb: the unforeseeable was none other than the renouncement itself, as though each event, in order to reach me, in that region where we were navigating together, had demanded of me the promise that I would slip out of my story. This, unfortunately, applied to everything and to the most simple things, those with which, at certain moments, I was prepared to be content. I may say that I had the day at my disposal, but on condition that it should not be this day and, even more, that this one should be in part forgotten, should be the sun of forgetfulness.

All else failing, the idea of assigning to him directly the means that he himself had put at my disposal or that had obliged me to have him at my disposal, to make a place for him that I could no longer measure: I would have liked him to give his opinion of such a plan. But to my surprise, he seemed to ignore my question completely. I must point out that, though he rarely spoke about himself, he gave as little impression as possible of neglecting the person speaking to him: he listened in silence, but in such a way that his silences were not inert, though no doubt slightly suffocating, as if they consisted in repeating in a more distant world, repeating exactly, syllable for syllable, everything one was trying to make him understand. At least—and in fact it did happen that his refusal to answer was not a refusal, but contributed to pursuing the conversation, to obliging it to prolong itself beyond all measure, to wear itself down to such a degree, through repetition and obstinacy, that it could only continue and continue on—if he did not answer, he also did not go on to another subject, for in some way he had to content himself with the paths I drew for him, I mean he no doubt felt he had done his duty sufficiently by giving me my cue. For the moment, he did not give it to me; on the contrary, he asked, as though to put me on the wrong track, and after a silence that increased the volume of the question: "Tell me, won't it be winter soon?"

To say that I stumbled over what he had said would not be saying much. I felt I was passing through one world after another. I could have absorbed myself in it for days, and perhaps I would have, if the thought that at no price should the thread be broken had not brought me back to the necessity of answering, unfortunately to question in my turn: "What winter are you talking about?"

"Well, ours, naturally."

"Ours?"

I remained suspended on that fascinating shared season: "Do you mean that I won't have enough time to..."

It was not that I was afraid to give a name to what I wanted to do, but I already saw his answer, the one that came back in the manner of a joyful promise and did not need much to be lured: "Oh, but you have all the time in the world."

But that answer did not come, and the one that came was in every respect astonishing:

"I mean: aren't you expecting company until then?"

Yes, it was astonishing, and this time I could not overcome

my astonishment, except to repeat: "Company? People?"—which led him to repeat, also: "People, people!" in a way that dismissed the conversation, that obliged me to consider that it would not resume except from a completely different source that I would now have to look for. I certainly had something to think about. But I had even more to be quiet about, and that was what was important: the possibility of remaining firmly in one spot, without moving.

I would have liked to think he could remain there too, for, even though he spoke of a place that seemed to be the center of the calm and even though he seemed at certain moments terribly restful, he was, in fact, restful in a terrible way. If I left him to himself, I did not forget him, but I soon lacked the strength to think of him, I was left with nothing but thought, and thinking was what could make our relations most sterile.

"Can I reflect on it?"

"Yes, of course. But for how long?"

"Oh, only a moment!"

He certainly didn't oppose it, but the fact that he added: "What shall we do while you're reflecting?" showed that he wanted to keep himself at a distance from "reflection" and that he didn't want to leave me entirely in it. I couldn't suggest to him that to reflect signified his distance, the faculty of interrupting motion by which what I said escaped me, hastened toward a strange point from which I wasn't sure I could make it come back. But the truth was that his distance really did signify reflection, and to hope to draw near him by dint of reflection did not put hope on a very good path. Nevertheless, I didn't abandon this path altogether. I could say where it was leading me: it was stagnation, empty perseverance, and even stupor, but starting from there, I imagined I had acquired enough heaviness to be able to go forward again, even though reflection consisted above all in repeating: You haven't reflected enough yet (you must become heavier). He himself was far from being without logic, he had a sort of fierce singleness of mind which, because it

9

apparently did not want to lead to anything, represented an almost formidable power, a power one couldn't combat except by suspiciously attributing to it goals, aims, and in this way an extraordinary muddle was developing whose approach, whose threat, I had sensed more than once. I could criticize myself severely for having so often, when faced with the sense of that power, sought refuge in reflection, by asking: "Can I reflect on it?"—which could only assure me "a moment," but at least that moment prevented the circle from closing, restrained me from closing it myself.

I didn't stay long in the place where I had arrived. The feeling of possessing something infinitely important went hand in hand with the impression that I wasn't taking advantage of it, and even though with use, the importance was almost surely destined to dissipate, I had no other way of keeping it alive. "Company, people"—I repeated these words, my words, to myself, words followed, with a joyful force, by his: "People, people!" without his ever betraying the desire to go farther. I couldn't hope to wear out his patience. I could wear out my own, I could wander from place to place, from window to window, to draw support from the outside, but this digression was futile, this coming and going took me back to the same point where I found him again, always more firmly anchored. In this I suffered a monstrous constraint. I may say that if I had little by little broken with everything, in fact this constraint itself signified the rupture, and I saw only too clearly that it had overcome my resistance, my will, but I had gained nothing by it, because for me defeat had taken the worst form by transforming my broken character into a stiffness impossible to wear out, an "I'm stopping here, I'm staying here" which paralleled, which confirmed, its own obstinacy. The fact that he had led me to break with everything, as though with the promise that now the field would be open to us, certainly represented the type of illusion for which I could not hold him responsible, but only myself. It is true that when I associated with company, he seemed to keep himself at a distance because of the company, and the need to put an end to an unfortunate duality, to avail myself of a single loyalty, a single truth, had little by little pushed me gently, ineluctably—where I was. As a result, company was lacking but the distance remained, even though there was nothing left to make us feel it, and, what was more, it didn't even remain, for it was only one of the forms of this open field which I alone was to roam. The strange thing was that at this very moment I believed I recalled what his words were alluding to and how they had to be answered, but this was also what I wanted to avoid, I wanted something else, I wanted it with a will that was weak, without capacity, without light, a will that was only an agitated flight through the house. There is a hunger that is unacquainted with hunger, and it was this that caused my silence, a silence equal to his, avid, a desert, whereas his seemed to be fullness and balance, but I lived in the desert. I remember a period when I would constantly ask him a question I could only address to him from the depths of my unconcern:

"Do you know that?"—to which he would respond:

"Yes, it's true, I know it very well," and from these answers I derived a joyful pleasure, a strange cheerfulness, the impression that this reduplication was not the frame of the memory but the opening of space. At present, I lacked unconcern, I remained silent. I certainly wanted him to speak, but not in order to say, as he so often did, almost at random: "Well, another day has passed, hasn't it?"—because for whom had it passed? I could have asked him this, but he couldn't have answered that it had passed for us: it would pass later, perhaps; as I waited, I bore the weight of it and I didn't bear the fruit of it. I couldn't help expressing my reservation:

"Passed? but for whom? I'm asking myself that."

"Ah! One can certainly ask oneself that."

I keenly pushed my advantage: "Why do you repeat that phrase?"

11

"Do I repeat it?"—and he seemed less surprised than eager to allow me, in turn, to repeat my protest, to lead me to intensify it a shade by saying: "Yes, you repeat it all the time. Yes, I'm tired of it and you ought to stop doing it"—words I kept to myself, and I was rewarded for that, in a way, because he made this remark:

"But it's to help you."

I tried to explain to myself why the word "help" directed such a sharp point at me, as though he had actually said to me:

"You know, I can do nothing for you but repeat that from time to time."

I didn't succeed in emerging from that feeling, and of everything useful I could have pointed out to him on this subject, all that occurred to me was this remark, which circumvented his own:

"That helps me?"

Which he answered right away with a joyful urgency that was also a reminder of his own fate:

"It helps both of us!"

"You too? You mean we're connected?"

He seemed prepared to study the question, but the examination promptly led to these words:

"Well, you know that very well!"—which were addressed to me in a tone that returned me to myself.

In fact, I didn't know it. I knew there was neither understanding nor community of interest nor anything that corresponded to the idea that we were connected. It only seemed to me that I was in control of that idea, and that as a consequence, I was a judge of the reality of those connections: it depended on me, it depended on me so completely that all that could be said about it was "you know that very well," so that it ought to have been easy to arrive at a certainty on this point, if one difficulty had not remained, which was that for my part, in fact, I did not know it. This feeling gave me the strength to ask him:

"It was a long time ago that we met, wasn't it?"

He seemed to want to measure this time, conscientiously, and the result was a long silence, an abnormally long silence, which seemed destined to fulfill my expectation, soothe it, and perhaps make me pronounce other words, but since I said nothing, he answered in a slightly disappointing way:

"It wasn't so very long ago..."

In the meantime, during this silence, I had changed my idea, and I formulated this new idea with real energy: "But everything depends on what is meant by the word 'meet.'"

He immediately agreed: "Yes! Everything depends on that."

I went on: "Perhaps it would be better to say that soon we will meet in earnest."

Which he confirmed without hesitation:

"Soon—I think so too."

"But," I continued, "isn't 'soon' 'now'?"

"That's it—now, whenever you like."

A dialogue which I felt was so disappointing, so uselessly closed only through my own fault and also through the fact that my words—and the same was true of his—could only return to their point of departure; why? if I had known that, a great burden would have been lifted from me. I imagined it had to do with time. After all, we were talking, but perhaps everything had been said, and what I went on saying was incapable of consuming any time, also incapable of stopping it, freezing it. But why had everything been said?—between us? This explained his way of being, his patience, and the feeling of distress that seemed to me the mark, the sincerity of our relations. When I alluded to a meeting, I could only be alluding to that "everything has been said" which was the truth of it, and it was quite immaterial, dangerously immaterial, whether it had taken place a long time ago or not so very long ago or even "then," a "then" that compromised the future, since all these words were only one of the forms of our meeting, forms whose choice was given up to me with a "whenever you like" whose cruel transparency I under-

13

stood. Then I made this remark, which showed how little importance I attached to my "reflections":

"Aren't we too close to each other now?"

But, as though to concede that I was right, he limited himself to asking in turn:

"Too close?"

"Yes," I said, "too close: I'm not thrusting you away, I probably wouldn't have the strength to, I don't have the desire to either. I mean that if this desire exists, it doesn't succeed in making a choice between you and me. Can I make this choice? That's the question I'm asking you."

He appeared astonished by this flood of words, whose disorderly and demanding quality made them seem more like the force of breathing than like words and, in fact—a coincidence I might have reflected upon—I noticed that the wind, as though it had taken over from them or as though I had found in its power the memory of my decision, had at that moment begun to blow, a harsh, cold wind, as often prevailed in those regions of the South. Even he appeared to notice it.

"At least," he said, "at least...."

I can't explain why those two words did me some good, perhaps they reduced my tension, perhaps they expressed to me something about his nature; I didn't linger over them for long, because he added:

"We want to be reasonable, we want to wait," and after a moment that marked something like his hesitation at a threshold:

"Isn't this house pleasant?"

I answered briefly: "Yes, it is."

My dryness didn't stop him from wanting to dig deeper into the ground, and "dig" expressed exactly, I believe, what he wanted: to find out what foundations we were built on:

"It is!" he said. "Would you find it tiresome to describe it to me—yet again?"

I have to confess that even though I understood the extraordinary assistance he was giving me, I was put on my guard by his last words, which almost mechanically forced me to answer:

"I can't do it."

But he didn't allow himself to be discouraged:

"Together we could do it."

"Together?"

"You know," he said with a sort of fervor, "I would like to do something for you, I would like to do everything for you."

"Everything?"

The silence that followed was equal to that "everything": I felt that I should sink into it, but what I also felt was that at the same time I should make everything around me that was still solid slide into it.

I must have remained in the same place for a long time (I was standing at the bottom of the staircase, but I probably sat down on one of the steps a little later). Because of this last cry, something of me had been taken from myself; I touched the outside more, I also touched it less, I looked at the room, which seemed to extend quite far, I couldn't see its limits very clearly, I remembered the space instead, as I remembered myself. I stood up to go to the kitchen for a glass of water, but I must have mistaken the door, I saw below me a dimly lit, disorderly room which I didn't have the strength to go down into (probably the storeroom).

I found myself again a little farther on. I heard a door bang, no doubt the one I must not have closed behind me, which the wind was flinging back. But this noise seemed very distant to me. Everything was extraordinarily calm. Looking out through the large bay windows—there were three of them—I saw that someone was standing on the other side; as soon as I noticed him, he turned to the window and, without pausing where I was, stared rapidly, with an intense but rapid gaze, at the whole expanse and depth of the room. I was perhaps in the center of it. I couldn't see clearly the garden that had to be outside, but I recalled it with great vividness, with a force that resembled desire. I could make out what was around it. While I was inside that image, I tried to look again, a little farther, to see if someone was still there, but I didn't succeed, or not altogether. Yet I remembered these words: "People, people," which led me to say, softly:

"I think someone is there."

"Someone? Here?"

"Just now someone was looking through the window."

"Through the window?"

Words spoken in a tone of voice so uncommon, so quiet, that I in turn began to feel a kind of fear. What frightened me was that he seemed to repeat my words without altogether understanding them, and this thought occurred to me: Does he know what a window is?

"Someone who was outside looking into the room."

"Here?"

"Where we are."

He said, again:

"Who was it?"

"I don't know, I didn't see him well enough."

"And did he see you?"

I reflected. I don't know why, but this question caused me some anguish; all I could say to him was:

"Perhaps he didn't see me, perhaps he didn't see anyone."

At that moment I felt a weariness—to use that word—that bore into space, that sought to substitute for it another, thinner space, an empty, rootless air. Yet I heard him go on to say to me:

"You know, we should remain alone, we are alone."

It may be that some time went by, a time that was also airless and rootless. I was still thirsty, I had sat down next to a table, and when I heard him murmur, "This is a moment that will pass," I confused those words with these others: "Another day has passed, hasn't it?"; and that memory made me shiver, something in me broke. I had endured so many struggles, I had been so far—and where was "so far"? Here, next to a table. Perhaps my silence, my immobility, and the feeling that a kind of balance had been established between us, restored some of my strength to me; perhaps, on the contrary, I had gained in weakness; at a certain moment, I found myself in the room again, and beyond the table, in the spot where I had said to myself that the end had to be situated, there was a wall and, I believe, a mirror, at least a lightly shining surface. I tried to recognize this spot—was this where I had just been? was this me? In any case, at present the person who happened to be there was also leaning on a table. Thirst, the need to exhaust the space, made me stand up. Everything was extraordinarily calm. Looking at the large bay windows—there were three of them—I saw that someone was standing on the other side; as soon as I noticed him, he turned to the window and, without pausing where I was, he stared intensely at the expanse and depth of the room. I was still next to the table, I wanted to turn around quickly to face this figure, but I was surprised that I was now very near the windows and yet felt I was still in the middle of the room. This forced me to look strangely at a point that was not given to me, closer than it seemed to me, close in an almost frightening way, for it did not take into account my own distance. While I looked for the figure almost randomly, I noticed, in a flash—a flash that was the shining, tranquil light of summer—that I was holding this figure against my eyes, a few steps away, the few steps that must still have separated me from the bay windows, and the impression was so vivid that it was like a spasm of brightness, a shiver of cold light. I was so struck that I couldn't help murmuring:

"Don't move, I think someone is there."

"Someone? Here?"

"Someone is looking at us through the window."

"Through the window?"

Words which immediately gave me a feeling of dread, horror, as though the emptiness of the window were re-

17

flected in them, as though all this had already taken place, and once again, once again. I think I cried out, I slipped or fell against what seemed to me to be the table. Yet I heard him say to me again:

"You know, there is no one there."

I retained a memory of this that resembled the space in which I stood up again a little later. Yet I was rational enough to lean on the table, slowly follow its edge, and in this way I went a little farther. It was now much darker, although the little daylight that remained had an exceptional reality, as if outside me. It was this daylight that held me firmly against the wall, did not allow me to move away from it, as though, according to it, all the danger, which also had the force of a ruinous desire, was situated somewhere more in the middle of the room. The path, a narrow margin, led me—where it wanted, to another spot, where I too, no doubt, wanted to be led, at another moment, but when I reached it, I thought right away that it was the kitchen I had already been looking for. What struck me was a little wall that divided it, a partition over which one's gaze passed joyously: it was like a reserve, an unexpected gaiety of space, an emptiness within an emptiness. The place had the gayest appearance, a brightness poured down into it which, in contrast to the place I had come from, evoked the most certain moment of the day, a midday freed of the seasons and the hours. A silent light, however, which, as I saw, entered through a small kitchen window. What struck me further was that here I recognized all the disorder of a life that was habitual to me: I must have eaten here, at this table, only a few moments before—a glass, a bottle, a pharmaceutical tube. As I recalled my thirst, I wanted to drink, but the bottle was empty.

The strength that had brought me this far deserted me at this moment. I asked him (this happened when I found myself in front of the table, with its disorder intact): "What do you think of this room?"

"It's nice."

"It's strange, isn't it?"

"No, it's nice."

"At the moment, you have two rooms at your disposal."

A remark which he greeted with good humor:

"I certainly expect to have others too."

"And I?"

"Well, you will have them along with me."

I didn't want to raise any objections, what I wanted took an unexpected form:

"Do you know where I was before I came here?"

"Yes," he said, "actually I know very well."

"So you don't think I've always been here?"

I tried to think about my question, which gave me such a breadth of uncertainty, such a depth of sadness and forgetfulness that I had to complete it, shortly afterwards, with this other one:

"Do you mean I've moved away, moved farther and farther away? but why? what could possibly have occurred? what has happened?"

"I wonder."

This phrase, a sort of parenthesis in which time circulated, struck me, even though he often used it, for it suddenly seemed to have a meaning I hadn't seen so clearly until now, and this induced me to add:

"Do you mean it hasn't happened yet?"

But I sensed it, my question came too late, it could only strike—gently—against the foggy presence of that remark, through which he reaffirmed himself, though not without apprehension:

"Yes, I wonder about that."

I tried, in turn, to wonder about it; for a moment I thought I was succeeding—and the place where I arrived was nothing less than that beautiful bright spot, the kitchen, for whose sake I had broken the silence and which I looked at now as though it had been the space open to the one who wondered about it. Was it here?

He didn't answer, but the silence closed on me again as though he had said: there is no "here" for such a pain. I felt it immediately, I was tied to that pain, it too had closed on me again, it had its space, its walls, its tranquil light. Yes, it was a peaceful summer, that pain, and perhaps it had brought me here, but "here," though everything in it seemed as completely motionless as in a place where nothing happens, could not be here. I remained here nevertheless. It seems to me that remaining was also what the pain wanted, and I believe I had the impression it needed me for that; but, at the same time, it drew me powerfully, with a strength I wouldn't be able to describe. I saw the door, slightly open: beyond, the darkness, the half-light, of the room, farther beyond, the center of the room. I must say, now, that I had this thought: that my companion knew more about it than I, it was possible, that he had relations with it that made me believe that with his help I could understand it better, make it even more transparent and myself more transparent in it, it was a diffuse manifestness, a tempting light toward which truth itself drove me, but nevertheless I could not unite them in myself, I couldn't do it; on the contrary, they seemed to me as unknown to each other as I was perhaps close to both of them. This was, in a way, the most terrible thing about it: one can't really disappear when one must die in two separate worlds. What added to the temptation to appeal to him was that since I was talking to him and he was answering me, I was ahead and in any case directed toward him, engaged in the promise he had put at the center of things, in a sense, by declaring to me that he "wanted to do everything for me," a promise by which I was so completely surrounded that it, too, was the space in which I was moving. Eventually I asked him:

"I spoke of you as a companion. Isn't that a thoughtless word?"

"I might be your companion? Whom did you say that to?"

"To myself, while I was reflecting."

"I don't think I'm behind that word, I think you shouldn't use it."

"But don't you remember what you promised me?"

"Do I remember it? Deeply, warmly—I wouldn't forget it so quickly."

I turned toward that reticence, it was not disappointing, but attractive, it was like a kind of timidity, perhaps because it slipped away into memory. It was this—I was not fooled by it—that committed me to going farther, to saying to him:

"Wouldn't it be more convenient if I could name you?"

"You would like to give me a name?"

"Yes, at this moment I would like to." And when he did not answer: "Wouldn't that make things easier? Don't we have to come to that?"

But he still seemed to be dwelling on his question:

"Give me a name? But why?"

"I don't know exactly: maybe to lose my own."

Which, strangely enough, caused him to recover his good humor:

"Oh, you won't get out of it that way!"

A reply which, I understood very well, summoned my own, awaited my own:

"But I don't want to get out of it."

And to avoid that expectation which sought to beguile in me words that had already been spoken, I had to make an effort that resulted in this question:

"Aren't there already many words between us?"

"Yes, certainly, many writings."

Then I remarked with some incoherence:

"You mean there shouldn't be any name between us?"

"Yes, that's it," but he added, with a lack of connection that showed that my own had not escaped him:

"You know, words should not frighten us."

Perhaps I didn't always realize it, since he unfailingly answered me with great good will, but to address him, hear him—and also to maintain our direction toward a goal I couldn't see, that I only sensed—took more strength than I had: a silent strength that assumed I had already freely abandoned my own and yet required of me—or was this a mistake, a trap?—the affirmation, reduced to the lightest transparency, that my presence was still maintained. I wasn't fighting against an adversary, nor was this a fight; I wasn't defending myself and I wasn't attacking anyone, no one was attacking me. If he had made my life an infinite torment and an infinite task, this was perhaps because of the infinite complicity I had constantly found in him, without being aware of it, I could only mention to him the limit I wanted to place in front of me: was this conversation going to stop abruptly yet again? hadn't I already said to him what I now had to answer him once more?

"I am tired of your presence."

"To such a point?"

"Yes, to such a point, to such a point, as you hear me say."

He let some time go by. I had the feeling he was preparing to say: "What should I do?"—and I was ready to turn that question around: "What can you do?"

But he skipped ahead oddly:

"Is it at this point that we should become connected in a more real way? You wish for something of that sort, don't you?"

I couldn't deny it, I had wished for it; when? just a short time before; perhaps I no longer wanted it now. But he took no notice of my hesitations:

"And you would like to be connected in order to be able to disconnect yourself too?"

Yes, I had also had that thought, but I had had to move away from it because of its form:

"It isn't as clear as that," and he confirmed this right away:

"That would be of little use to us, that would stop us pointlessly."

"Stop us?"

"Yes, but pointlessly."

22

I was close to admitting this, perhaps too quickly, for, as though to keep me on that slope of agreement, he said to me with an intimacy, an impetuosity, that was almost crazy:

"You have drawn me to you in a powerful way: aren't you speaking, aren't you hearing me? Isn't our element the same? What do you want? To leave this element?"

I could only say to him:

"When you speak that way, I feel closer to you."

"Close to you, close to what is close to you, not to me."

"Not to you? And yet," I said desperately, "you have just pointed it out — I'm speaking to you."

"You're speaking!" he cried brusquely in a tone of incredible scorn that seemed to me to come from a different mouth— oh, from an infinite past. I was tied to the spot.

As far as I could understand, I heard—and no doubt almost immediately—the shock of a muffled sound, the powerful banging of a door. The wind! That thought carried me out of the room in a motion I was only aware of when I found myself in a darker spot. I was seized by an immense need to act. The insistence, the return of the wind exercised an obvious authority over me. This need expressed the empty haste of the outdoors, responded to an appeal, a need to wander that falsified and confused space. It was a sort of rest: far from here, far from here and yet here. I could just as well have believed I was in a deserted place—but there was a difference I tried to perceive; I did not strain at it, I saw it well enough to be fascinated by it: it was that if I moved here and there, if at present I impersonally performed my tasks— I had turned on the lights, I had closed the door to the storeroom—this possibility of wandering, this work meant that somewhere, elsewhere, I had in fact been "tied to the spot." But when? For the moment, I could hardly think about it, I didn't even feel any disturbance, or only a slight impersonal uneasiness, as though, for me, fear was the fear that I risked causing in someone else. Yes, I recalled his reply, the violence of his repudiation, by which he had apparently tried

23

to break me, but I could not "take it badly," I could only acknowledge that he was right, I who alone was still right, and exactly what had happened? Surely, this went farther back; surely, when this had been said, something quite different had come to light through this remark, had sought a way out, something older, dreadfully old, which had perhaps even taken place at all times, and at all times I was tied to the spot. This seemed to me to explain why I could now come and go in this room, doing the things one habitually does—I had opened a cupboard, I ate quickly, then, when I was finished, I went to draw the curtains over the large bay windows. In any case, I had the feeling that I was less mistaken about all these motions, about the person performing them, who, now, was climbing the stairs and, I imagine, going to bed. To see him disappear was not, properly speaking, strange, since it was myself. But I cannot hide the fact that there was nevertheless something anguishing about this disappearance, something I couldn't control: he seemed so impersonal, he seemed to forget with such severity what he left behind him, forbidding himself to know whether, if he now entered that room, a room which opened off the bend in the staircase, in order to go to sleep like everyone else, this really happened because somewhere else he was tied to the spot.

Yet I couldn't sleep. The wind had become the violence, the distress of the wind, but it was not that powerful noise from outdoors that kept me awake, it was, on the contrary, the amazing calm that such a noise left intact. I couldn't be mistaken about this calm: it was like a place reserved within a place, which nevertheless was not situated here, which I thought I would be more likely to find by going backwards, by wandering, but I also couldn't reach it, for if I had the right to speak of the one who had "disappeared" in the third person, it was nevertheless myself, who was here and remained here. I couldn't say that he slept, I felt his reserve, his muteness, which accepted the night and, through the night,

riveted space to a single spot, whereas perhaps I could neither stop speaking nor withdraw. I persuaded myself that he
was, "for his part," even more inaccessible than I to my
companion—the one who did not recognize himself behind
that word—more of a stranger and in some sense removed
from his element; I persuaded myself of this precisely in
feeling his reserve, the fact that even his motions did not
speak. A reserve that seemed terrible to me, at that moment,
as anguishing as his disappearance, to which it was surely
connected, as though he had distanced himself, obliterated
himself, in the impersonal existence, in the extreme distress
that is not even that of someone, and although the right to
speak of myself in the third person seemed to me justified by
such an obliteration, I must acknowledge that speaking of
him caused me an infinite uneasiness, a frightful sadness,
with the feeling that this reserve deserved better, called for
a silence that unfortunately resisted, even though it seemed
to be the slope that invited me—me too—to slide down to it.
This was why, in that night in which I heard only my own
thought, to which nothing responded but that reserve which,
nevertheless, was none other than myself, I promised myself
to keep the secret of that "third person" at least from my
companion, even while asking myself if I would have enough
strength for it, if the secret did not mean that I lacked this
strength.

But what is one night? The next day, I got up as usual. "As
usual" was an expression that came to me from outside, a
sort of open window in that closed space. All night I had
wanted this moment: to get up and for everything to be as
usual. I couldn't have expressed exactly what this desire
meant: a need to lean on the world? a concern to verify the
day? to recognize appearances? I believe I humbly hoped to
have the strength to get up. That happened, and more easily
than I had hoped, above all more quickly. I had only time to
say to myself:

"How fast all this is happening! What, is it day?"

25

Which was echoed by the old remark:

"Another day has passed, hasn't it?"

I turned around toward him, and something of my sympathy, my gesture of confidence and welcome must have touched him, for when I said to him spontaneously: "Last night was infinitely long," I heard him answer me with a sort of delicacy:

"Wouldn't it be best not to move from here?"

"But I've already moved," I gaily pointed out to him.

"Then let's go," he immediately added, without further specifying the spot we should go to.

I climbed the steps, I went into a small toilet. On the same level, and a little later, opening the door I thought was the door to the stairway—but it must have been contiguous to it—I was in some sense attracted by the surprise, pierced and drawn by that surprise, which resembled the gaiety of the day, the shiver of a light so startling that, as I moved forward in that little room, it made me enter the heart of summer, and was I moving forward? it was the space that was opening, a limitless space, a day without hindrance, free, and that freedom, even though it was not without coldness—for I was immobilized in a feeling of radiant emptiness—was like the floating fantasy of summer. I assuredly recognized that little room where I didn't doubt I had spent a good deal of time and which, at that instant, gave me the impression of a watchtower, open on two sides, but empty (not that it was empty of objects, I now noticed a table), and yet empty to a degree that was exalting and, I fear, difficult to sustain. I think there was also a couch, for it seemed to me that I lay down on it, and when fatigue, the burden of that instant, threw me back against the wall, I continued to see the room in all its expanse, in its empty, uninhabited, and yet very cheerful presence. I can imagine that I kept silent for quite a long time. A little after, I came and sat down at the table. I was certain that I had already sat down there, and perhaps it had been just a short time before, perhaps now: the disturbance I felt came from the fact that in some way I myself was finding myself there again, and the thought that I was there, tied to the spot, immediately seized me again with an overwhelming force, at once more hopeless and more sterile than when it had struck me before. I couldn't help saying to him:

"I have the impression this is where I live."

"Are you sure?"

"I find this room strange."

"No, it's fine."

Certainly it was, and extraordinarily agreeable, as attractive as though all the movement of space were concentrated here in order to make it a burning beginning, the site of an encounter in which there was no one and in which I was not myself. Once again I had to let myself be drawn along by that impression.

A little later, I found myself back on the bed. Nothing was different: I still saw the table, it extended from one window to the other, from west to east, as far as I could tell. What struck me, what I tried to bring out of my musings, was why, in this little room, the impression of life was so strong, a radiant life, not of another age, but of the present moment, and mine—I knew it with a clear, joyful knowledge—and yet that clarity was extraordinarily empty, that summer light gave the greatest feeling of distress and coldness. This is open space, I said to myself, the vast country: here I work. The idea that I lived here—that I worked here—meant, it is true, that at this moment I was only here as an image, the reflection of a solitary instant sliding through the immobility of time. A cold thought I could not break down, that pushed me back, threw me back against the wall, just as "here" changed into "far from here," but that distance immediately became the radiance of the day, the soaring and the happiness of all of space burning, consuming itself to the transparency of a single point. What a vision! but, alas, only a vision. Yet I felt myself powerfully connected to that instant and in some sense under its domination, because of this my master,

27

in the impression that here a sovereign event was taking place and that to live consisted for me in being eternally here and at the same time in revolving only around here, in an incessant voyage, without discovery, obedient to myself and equal to sovereignty. Yes, this was the highest degree of life and even though, through this life, I had strayed into a deadly calm and a deadly solitude, I could say: it must be, it must be—I draw you to myself in a powerful way.

I can imagine how much time that lasted. I recall that after I left the little room—I left it because in reality I could no longer endure that moment, which meant, as I knew, that that moment could not endure me—as I was going away (I was going down the stairs) the feeling came to me, touched me, that I had gotten out just in time, but I was not fooled by the freedom I was thus giving myself, even if it resembled this remark: "You should go look downstairs and see if you're there," a remark as light as I myself, and that lightness expressed my aimless steps, the movement that drove me from one room to the other, while the doors banged and the wind slid joyfully behind space, at the level of the calm and the silence.

Downstairs, however—at the bottom of the staircase—I had to stop. Here I had stopped before, and the conviction that now I had to confront something, perhaps a task, seemed connected to this stopping. I recognized the darker day, although at this moment it was almost bright, the silence too, which was not greater than in the spot I had come from, but a little different, poorer, more desolate, as though it lacked something it needed to be a real silence, just as it seemed that only the presence of someone could transform it into a true solitude. Little by little I had this presentiment: that here, in relation to this place, I was burdened with a responsibility I could not turn away from, that obliged me to remain behind, as though to wipe out footsteps or begin over again what had not been done; yes, I had to respond to a role that I did not know, but that I could not disregard, that was more intimate with me than I myself and the burden of which I accepted as I momentarily gave it this name: responsibility toward solitude, deliverance to captive images.

I must confess that I would have liked to go on. Why this task? Why did it fall on me? Why had I come in here? Who was stopping me from leaving? Who was holding me back? No one, less than I, believed in the truth of a task, no one who was more alien to a duty, whatever it was. And can one call by the name of "duty" what is not due to anyone? "Responsibility" what dissipates in the absence of a response? A task, but one that can't be grasped, a demand, but empty, gloomy, and devastating, and yet a task, a responsibility, a duty. I could only turn to my companion, the one who was not accompanying me, and say to him: "I know what's going to happen, I know exactly. I will describe to you where I am, I believe I can trust you?"

"Yes, I think so, but on condition that I can also trust you."

"You mean that I should describe things to you as I see them?"

"As I would like to see them, as I would see them," and he added: "Yes, everything depends on that."

I reflected on that, it opened new horizons to me. I would have liked to make him understand how much what he was asking of me with such simplicity went beyond everything, exceeded my means, exceeded me, but out of fear that he would yield to my reasons and because I felt, with all the force of what was manifest, that in fact "everything depended on that," I chose to answer him:

"Yes, that's clear, that's what I should do, even if I can't do it. Listen, at this moment I'm at the bottom of the staircase, almost right up against the steps, on the other side and quite near me there is an armchair, but I'm not looking at it, because I'm turned toward the room that lies a little farther on. You see how things are?"

"More or less. It's dark, isn't it?"

"It isn't very dark, it's the day that is dark. You know,

29

everything is extraordinarily calm."

Yes everything was extraordinarily calm. Even he must have sensed that it was already too late, for he said softly:

"Stay where you are, don't move."

I wouldn't have been able to move, but what he was asking of me was no doubt something else: to confine myself to that moment of description, to keep it empty at all costs, to preserve it, prevent it from drifting—toward what could not fail to happen. I think I made a slight motion or tried to shift, but I ran up against my own immobility, and I immediately had the full sensation that in the armchair very near me—it was the proximity that was insane, for my hand, almost without moving, could have brushed against it—someone was sitting, someone I now perceived in a profound, intense way, even though the form was absolutely motionless, slightly bent over, but I didn't see it directly, for it was a little behind me. This lasted for one marvelously tranquil and profound instant, after which I said to him quickly:

"For a moment now, someone has been sitting here, in the armchair."

Right away, I was shaken, pierced, not because I felt the insane proximity of this presence, this intense, living, yet unmoving nearness: I could endure that, it seems to me I had always endured it; but the words themselves, from which I had expected some help to come, at the very least another sort of light, myself and reality stepping back; instead opened me up to the shiver of manifestness that formed the depth of that presence, made it ungovernable—inexplicably, absolutely human and yet absolute. And when he asked me: "Someone? Here?" the fact that I was awaiting his words, the shiver that ran behind them, enveloped them in a fear that he seemed to feel, a fear that drove that instant back toward another sort of time, older, fearfully old—all of this moved forward silently, expressed that image, seemed to take possession of it, then swerved toward this question:

"Who is it?"

"I don't know."

"Have you ever seen him before?"

"I don't think so"—but then this was suddenly torn from me: "Yes, I have seen him before."

It seemed obvious to me that he himself had drawn me there, that he had at least forced me to come to that word, to illuminate the visible side of an instant against which I had stood firm—I mean, with which I had lived side by side silently and in a manly way without its being able to come near. Now everything was said, at least at that second I had the violent, splendid certainty of it, which dissipated almost at the same moment, as soon as he asked me:

"When did you see him?"

I had to move away, for now I saw to my left the whiteness of a door that was sunk in the floor: the door to the storeroom, probably. I think I wanted to reach the table that was much farther on, beyond the center of the room, but as I was going around another armchair, I suddenly noticed a bed or a couch, but a remarkably broad and vast one, occupying one whole area of the room. The fact that I had not yet paid any attention to it struck me sharply; with joy I thought: one never sees everything in a room. I remained very surprised by the impression of immense tranquillity given off by that sight, it seemed to me I had never before noticed such a calm surface, such a restful, even, and silent expanse. I imagine I looked at that bed for quite a long time. I can't say the idea of lying down on it didn't occur to me; on the contrary, I felt the liveliest desire to do that, a desire that also took this form: that in that spot, I would have a completely different perspective on the room, a possibility of describing it that cheered me, delighted me infinitely, as though this would have been a friendly trick to play on my old companion. However, I did not lie down on it and I don't believe I really considered doing it. It didn't seem entirely possible to me. Why? I can't say exactly: the thought that I was here, but only by chance, because of a misfortune of time and also because somewhere else I was tied to the spot—and perhaps in the kitchen or upstairs, in the little room, the watchtower, where my musings evoked the image of the watchman, of the one who lives in the day and bears its weight—this thought now disappeared into another, that here I had to confront something, a task, a responsibility, but at this moment, what seized me again with an amazing intensity was the sensation of my immobility, of the certainty that once again kept me in that spot. There was no movement I could have made. Where I was, without turning around, I could see the steps, there were six or seven before one reached the sort of vault, rather low and heavy, under which the staircase made a turn. Now, the perception of what I saw brought a response to my companion. The figure was over there, I saw it motionless, almost turned away, as it seemed to me, and I had the feeling that at the moment my eyes were fixed on it, it was preparing to climb the last steps and disappear. This movement, which was not carried out, gave that presence a new truth, and the whole distance that separated us, measuring a few steps, made it astonishingly close, closer than a short time before when, as I realized, what made its insane proximity apparent was the distress of its distance. But the strangest thing was that in the space at that confined spot—and the form was, I saw, almost leaning against the wall—even though it couldn't see me and probably knew nothing of me, it was nevertheless stopped and suspended under my gaze, as though the fact that my gaze was riveted to it had, in fact, riveted it to that point. There was something odd, absolutely unhappy about that, and I was so shaken by it that the background of strangeness against which this scene was unfolding was transformed. Probably, affected by my disturbance, I must have moved slightly: now I saw the staircase from a steeper perspective, rising abruptly toward the figure I was still staring at, which revealed itself more, so that the impression I had was that of someone larger than I had thought, yes, it was this feeling that struck me then, of someone a little larger than he should have been, and I don't know why this singularity was like a disconcerting summons to my eyes, an insistence that maddened my gaze and prevented its grasping anything. It seems to me that I was prepared to approach even closer, perhaps to bring this moment back to life, to allow it to reconquer itself; but what happened and what I could have foreseen, actually struck me as unexpected—I believe I had never forgotten him to this degree before—and, when he asked me: "Do you see him at this moment?" I, in my surprise and also because of a sort of pain that I felt spring up in me, faced with this speech, which sought to encroach on me and participate in a guarded moment, did not answer, no doubt incapable. Shortly after, from very far away, from the distance that was made of my resistance and my disavowal, I heard him murmur:

"You know, there's no one there."

I don't know if I welcomed the remark at that moment, but at that moment, with extreme emotion, I saw the figure visibly move a little, I saw it slowly climb a step, approach the turn, and enter the area of shadow.

Among all the impressions I had, I think the strongest was this: that the evidence of reality had never been as pressing as in this slip toward disappearance; in this movement, something had been revealed that was an allusion to an event, to its intimacy, as though, for this figure, to disappear was its most human truth and also the truth closest to me. And the other feeling I had was the counterpart of such a certainty: the disheartening but also radiant emptiness expressed for me by this disappearance, an event I was not even tempted to ascribe directly to what my companion had said. I won't say I saw no connection between these two signs, but I sensed a deeper, more imposing interdependence, that of two spheres that didn't know each other, two moments in time perhaps entirely foreign to each other and coming together within their shared foreignness. Which had come before the other? He had now uttered that remark, but "now" had perhaps already happened in the past, was repeating itself, was taking place again—again? but it couldn't take place again, and everything returned to being empty and lifeless. This feeling expressed, at that point, the desperate movement I was making and that perspicacity could only cause to be infinite. Yes, it had already taken place, and the question of knowing just when was a futile one, the certainty of remembering a matter of indifference, for it seemed to me that I belonged, not to the order of things that happen and that one remembers with joy or sadness, but to the element of hunger and emptiness where what does not take place, because of that, begins again and again without any beginning or any respite.

I did not deny that I would have done anything, given up anything, to be able to get out of there, and yet the certainty that I couldn't, despite my desire and despite appearances, was enveloped in this idea: which was that I had to stay there, keep standing there, this was my task, the beginning of a decision I had to sustain by remaining always on my feet, betraying it as little as possible, without ever being relieved of myself, but always confronting a demand that gave me the feeling I myself had also disappeared and, far from thinking I was more free of it, that I was connected by this disappearance, connected ever more closely to it, of being called, sworn to sustain it, make it more real, more true and, at the same time, push it farther, always farther, to a point truth can no longer reach, where possibility ceases. I saw the terrible, deceptive aspect of such a thought, I fought against it, and it did not resist, its lightness left me free, became the transparency I couldn't rip apart without harming a free moment. At certain times, it seemed to me this transparency was the only solid ground that still remained to me and, if I went forward, it was by resting on it, on my own image thus reflected, while this reflection was perpetuated to infinity, indifferent to the ruins of time. A reflection that had no doubt attracted me by its fragility, the assurance that in resting on it I would inevitably fall fast, but the fall was infinite, at each moment of the fall the reflection formed again under my steps, indestructible. I would also sometimes feel, and precisely at that moment, that this task—a word I would have liked to choose to be even more insignificant, emptier, and, because of that, more appropriate to its imperious power—this demand was the bond that joined me to myself, to the one who had lived in the small room, close to the daylight and bearing its weight. Perhaps I was necessary to him, and no doubt such a necessity weighed on me as much as one can be heavy to oneself, but I also sensed that he was placing a certain hope in me, that this task and this burden were related to that expectation. What was he expecting? I did not know. Could it have been that the strange distance established between us, through which, as I clearly saw, entered the infinite torment that was my space and my air and my days, could it have been that this distance, interior and yet measured by the reality of a few moments, yes, the fact that I was a little on this side, a little behind, in this strangely perilous, but strangely attractive region of the reflection—did this immense separation give me a sort of release? But why this suspense, this pause? I couldn't see all this clearly, and this darkness also had the weight of my task and my responsibility, for I too, in my own way, was looking for the daylight, even if I had to be content with an errant, imprisoned gleam, the scintillation of an instant, which I sometimes almost preferred to the light of the world. Yes, I said to myself, my part is the best—for my part, I am here, I'm staying here.

Which he did not fail to answer:

"But you have all the time in the world."

I noticed, then, that I had reached the table, whose round surface I saw turning about an empty vase, and even though I had had the impression of having fallen there, I was calmly seated, which did not prevent me from thinking: what a shame I didn't fall on the bed, whose peaceful image remained in my mind. I didn't feel very tired, but rather disoriented, prodigiously without any work to do, and this being without work was also my task, it occupied me: perhaps it represented a dead time, an interval of abandonment and faintness on the part of the watchman, a weakness that obliged me to be alone, myself, but the empty disturbance in which I was moving about had to have another meaning, evoked hunger, evoked a need to wander, to go farther, by asking: "Why did I come in here? am I looking for something?" whereas I was perhaps not looking for anything and "farther" was still here and here, at each instant. This I knew. Knowing formed part of that solitude, formed that solitude, was at work in my being without work, closed the ways out. In my lack of work, I asked him:

"Do you know what happened just now?"

"Yes, I know very well, but do you want us to talk about it? Is that a good thing? We must be reasonable."

"It may not be a very good thing, but I'm not really speaking either. You remember, you pointed that out to me."

"Do I remember? Profoundly, amicably; you were struck by it."

"I didn't take it badly. I, too, think we aren't really talking: one can't call this speech."

Which led him to say to me:

"Is that what you're thinking now?" but he didn't leave me the time to explain it, for without transition he went on to this certainty:

"Oh, we understand each other perfectly!"

As I was reflecting on this assurance, he suddenly asked me with a strange voracity:

"Are you writing? Are you writing at this moment?"

A question that chilled me, as though there had been a lack of taste on his part in this, a dog snuffling at its own smell.

"I don't do it at night, at this time of year. It's already cold."

"And the summer?"

"Yes, in the summer, sometimes."

He firmly continued his inquiry:

"And do you read?"

"Not much, not as much as I should."

"Why don't you read?"

I must admit I was shaken by the seriousness and the passionate interest of his questions: Why wasn't I reading? I asked myself, and from that question sprang an answer I gave him rather joyfully:

"I would rather converse with you," which he, too, accepted joyfully, by repeating:

"Oh, we understand each other perfectly."

But perhaps not as well as he would have liked, for his reply took him back to mine, which he seemed to turn around:

"Yes, we are conversing with each other," and the silence that resulted from this emerged from that dislocated remark, revealed its fault, its cleft, which disturbed me painfully. In myself, I said to myself:

"Now let's see what you're worth," and I thought to prove to myself what I was worth by declaring brusquely to him:

"You know, I trust you, except on one point, because there really was someone here, just now."

"Really?"

"Yes, really, really."

I understood the risk I was running by affirming this reality in front of him like that, but something drove me to maintain it whatever the cost, it seemed to me I owed the credit for it to an event which I should not allow to be obliterated, which I would otherwise never be able to go back to, and which also needed this indefinitely maintained assurance in order to realize itself. I wanted to make him understand that on this point I wouldn't yield, I wouldn't deny my certainty. In fact, my conviction didn't seem to find him alien to it, only disconcerted, and at that moment I leaped at the thought that I had perhaps forgotten certain details, that there was a lacuna through which reality had escaped, that I had, for example, neglected to describe to him the armchair that I could see by lifting my eyes, though it was in the depth of the room, quite far from me, it is true, and even farther from him: a sturdy country chair that sometimes reminded me of Van Gogh's. The fact that someone was sitting there, in that armchair, had a humble truth to it, the truth of this very cramped place, and I could only reflect inexhaustibly on that truth, of which so little remained to me, for it didn't even signify repose, an attitude of repose, but equally well indifference to repose. Perhaps he discerned what he took to be a doubt, though it was, on the contrary, the torment of a certainty reduced to itself alone; he asked me softly:

"Who was it?"

"I don't know." But he didn't forget that I had said more to him, and he made me feel it in his next question:

"Did he see you?"

I thought about it, and I felt the anguish, the sadness, that recalled to me the presence of that figure, riveted to a single point by the fact that I was riveting it with my gaze: it was no longer more than that point, then, an empty, silent point, an empty moment that had become tragically foreign to my gaze at the very moment when my gaze became the error of what rivets, and my gaze itself was empty, did not enter that zone, entered it without reaching it, encountered only the emptiness, the closed circle of its own vision. Upon which he insisted:

"What was he like?"

"I don't think I want to describe him to you, at least not now. It seems to me I shouldn't."

"You mean you could?"

"I don't think I should ask it of myself."

"Ah!" he said strangely, "I see, I see, you respect him." And when I did not deny it, he abruptly changed the subject, and this new subject was revealed by these words:

"Aren't you afraid of it? Isn't it a frightening association?"

The word "frightening" startled me, bewildered me. All of a sudden I saw it with a force that, in fact, did not leave me intact: what had been there was frightening, was what I could not associate with, and in this slipping, it seemed to me that I myself could no longer associate with anyone, not even with myself. Was it such a feeling of rupture that caused me to be a stranger to that instant, provoked a fall, a dizziness in which, far from repelling the frightening association, I found myself close to it, joined to it by sympathy, by a desire to recognize it? A movement that made me travel through abysms and yet more abysms, and I could have believed someone was there, because what I felt was so like the shiver of his approach. I was so illuminated by this that he, too, had to believe in his presence, and he quickly asked me:

"Do you see him at this moment?"

But this question showed me that the light I had just travelled through wanted to illuminate something quite different, the very answer I gave him at that moment in all its "light":

"Yes, I have seen him before."

A mad thing to say, and as soon as it slipped out, it seemed the most dismal thing that could happen to me, the cowardly impulse that had caused me to replace the disconcerting with the familiar, and, out of a desire to master the unknown, with the already known. And yet, could I reject such a light? Had I not, for an instant, been on intimate terms with that absence, so close to it that to see it would have disrupted the intimacy? But that speech .... We listened to it, of course, both of us, and he didn't allow it to move away:

"You mean you saw him somewhere else, somewhere different from here?"

Under the tension imposed on me by his question, I slid into a remark about him that I could have been tempted to make to myself earlier, if I hadn't been so little tempted to approach him through remarks: which was that I felt bound

39

to be all the more frank the more discreetly he existed—if I didn't want to reduce that errant speech of mine, which I rejoined at certain moments in time and at certain points in space, to the whimsicality of an echo, I could not forget to treat it with an infinite seriousness, equal to its infinite complicity and patience. But while I was building myself a rampart out of my "remarks," he did not deviate in any way from his direction, as I had hoped, he even affirmed it still more vigorously by adding:

"You mean you know him?"

This made me realize that it would be best to answer:

"I thought I recognized him, but when you ask me that question, I'm convinced that I don't know him in any way befitting that word." I added: "You know very well what I mean."

Loyally, he acknowledged it: "I know."

But listening to him, it occurred to me that perhaps he didn't know it in the same way I did, even though he drew a surprising answer from it:

"And just now, was it the same each time?"

It did not take me long to understand him; he wanted to take back from me a little more than I had given him, and perhaps he left me my certainty, but on condition that it be insignificant, yes, severely deprived of meaning and truth. I was drawn into a path where I only stopped to ask him:

"You mean I'm not always the same?" Which at last showed me where I was going.

I think I was exhausted with bitterness, my courage failed me. I had endured so many struggles, I had been so far, and where was "so far"? Here, by this table, whose surface, too, I saw turning with the lightness of an empty movement, and the person who happened to be there was perhaps writing, and, as for me, I was leaning on him, on me someone else was leaning, on that person, yet another: at the far end of the chain, there was still this room and this table. There was nothing I could lean on in the face of such an infinity, I was without strength in the face of the emptiness the question kept opening and closing, so that I could not even fall into it. Rather, it uplifted me, uplifted me with exhaustion, and I think that when I saw myself standing, that movement, that desperate need to exhaust space caused me to fling at him in response, with a suddenness in which was mustered the resolve I made at that moment:

"I will continue to go in this direction, never in any other."

For me, "in this direction" no doubt indicated where he was, the interminable, the place where the moments led me back to such a point of uncertainty and sterility that what had preceded them was obliterated, that they themselves were obliterated. Infinite moments, which I could not master, and the most terrible thing was that, as a constant pressure, I felt the duty to make myself their master, to orient them, to transmit to them that pressure, which sought to make them slide toward an end to which they could not consent. I could not entirely resist this pressure, this imperious narration, it was inside me like an order, an order that I was giving myself, that unsettled me, dragged me along, obliged me to wander. I could not avoid the thought, then, that this pursuit was not mine alone, my error, but that it was also present around me, in the intimacy of space, in the secrecy of that speech, that called to the emptiness and did not find it, or that wanted to recover itself and could not.

Since I was coming and going—at a distance, certainly, but still here—I could not neglect what was happening here, or I, too, had to live according to the truth of negligence, in which, even while adhering to the transparent vision of the day, I found no less important the emptiness of the reflections surrounding me at every instant, and even more: things happened in such a way that, even while seeing them happen infinitely at a distance and farther from me than I ever could have reached, I felt intimately responsible for them. I think that I will express an aspect of the truth, in the language he chose, by saying we understood each other. This understanding was perhaps infinitely strange to me, but even when it escaped me, when I was still outside it, I did not forget it, I continued to feel directly responsible for it, in my uneasiness, doubt and also foreboding, foreboding that was empty, infinitely without happiness but stubborn, demanding, for, without contact with the instant that I had to sustain, and not immobilize, but leave free, even while going to meet it, I was obliged, in the ignorance of an empty foreboding, to give proof of understanding and creative alliance and yet not be concerned about all this, lest the time of the concern come to dislocate the understanding and miserably torment the emptiness.

I can't express myself any other way. It seems to me that in my disarray, in which I had to fight against the interminable and yet lift it up to the daylight, forbid myself to be anxious, in search of an instant that did not want to be sought and that nevertheless desired it, in that space whose resemblance I had to sustain, I applied all my strength to remaining connected to myself. Perhaps this was a mistake, perhaps what I called faithfulness and seriousness, the will to remain on my feet, was only a narrow aspiration to remain, a prayer addressed to the night asking it to linger a little while longer. Yes, it's possible, but one can't deliberately give up contenting oneself, one can only fight to maintain the rigor of a form and contact with the day. Go up, go down, but even in the shadows and as far as possible, one must fight for transparency.

I didn't forget it, the world is based on itself and the earth alone is the seat of the gods. From this, too, came the heavy feeling of my responsibility, the seriousness with which I had to approach myself, follow myself in the trial that obliged me to live short of myself, in the intimacy of wandering, in that understanding with something I could not entirely un-

42

derstand and which I had to sustain firmly, without removing myself from it, and, insofar as I could, without straying.

I had many proofs that we understood each other, but this one in particular made me reflect: when I ceased to be alone, solitude became intense, infinite. There was nothing strange about that truth, it only made the spot where I was staying prodigiously true, the spot I found to be in all aspects like itself, like the description of it produced at this same spot or sometimes elsewhere—the description of it, of all that happened here and that asserted itself here. This resemblance was prodigious, it did not have the incisiveness, the authority of obviousness, rather it was a prodigy, it seemed gratuitous, unjustified, incontestable, but not sure, of a reality more interior and yet all in appearance, all contained in visible splendor, and to come and go, there, was a delight from which I could remove myself all the less because I had the happiness of seeing things in the gaiety of their solitude, which did not take my presence into account, which played with my absence and, it is true, the word "understanding" also had the cheerfulness of a game about which we understood each other. I think the solitude was best expressed by that gaiety: a light laugh of space, a fund of extraordinary playfulness that did away with every reservation, every alternative, and which resonated like the emptiness of an echo, the renunciation of mystery, the ultimate insignificance of lightness. Perhaps I wouldn't have noticed it if he hadn't suddenly asked me:

"Why are you laughing?"

A question that forced me to reflect, for I was not laughing at all, I was, rather, within the musing that had followed my resolve, hardly in a very happy state of mind. A striking question, posed to me, it seemed, at a decisive moment that did not correspond to my state of mind, that evoked another question, another day, and, what was more, I was startled every time he showed he was capable of coming to me by a path I had not laid out. I could have asked him what the object of his question was, but I found this answer myself:

"Because I'm not alone."

Which he translated in his own way:

"Is it that you're not here?"

I took it cheerfully:

"Do you want to know where I am? I've just drawn back the curtains of the large bay windows, and I'm looking out." There I rediscovered, joyfully preserved, the little garden— hardly a garden, a few feet of earth enclosed within walls— which lay just in front of me, a little beyond the panes, beyond but within my reach, so that by looking outside, I also had the feeling of touching the depths of a memory, its last chance, so much did that little area extend me, give me a little more than I should have received, which, because of that, I received twice over. Once again I remembered the pleasure it had always brought me and, even at present, I was startled by this unexpected possibility, this reserve of space and light toward which I was still allowed to turn. This was not the splendor of limitlessness, such that, there where I lived and worked, in the little room, brightness gave it to me to contemplate as the unique moment and sovereign intensity of the outside. Here, there was nothing but a little fragment, something as joyful as a real shrub planted in the heart of a dream. Which I saw—but at that instant I had the impression that what I saw was cruelly lacking to him. I was also struck by the loyalty that permitted me to keep him at a distance, never to think that he could play his game alone. Which quickly led me back to my answer, over which, I then saw, he had remained poised, without taking notice of my contemplation, and I received his own answer once again:

"It's true, you're not alone, but we are alone."

That "we" impressed me, appeared to have a different tone. It seemed to me that before he spoke he had withdrawn from my vicinity, had exiled himself, and this exile became the basis of the understanding, whence, then, like a breath exhaled, the life of the speech, worn, burned, yet strangely alive, was expressed. The "we" appeared to me to be an allusion to that exile, to the fascinating need to distance himself under the pretext of coming close, and it occurred to me that if I had to expend such strength in these conversations, it was because I first had to distance him, distance myself from him, and the greater the distance was, the more profound and true the speech was, like everything that comes from far away. This was not the tranquil delay, the suspension that I granted myself so often while "reflecting": it was a silent, powerful struggle, but also scarcely real, a dream movement, in which I had to deprive myself of life, abstain from myself, so as to make all approaches useless to him and allow him to give voice to the distance. But was this how it was? What I have just called exile did not evoke separation, but return, presence in the shining world of negligence, and perhaps the effort I was making consisted in opening up, everywhere I happened to be, an interval that was his dwelling place, in erecting the tent of exile where I could communicate with him—because he was not there. But was this how it was? I catch myself imagining that if he withdrew from my question, he never withdrew completely and, in this apparently open field, he left a remnant, as the day does in the night, a simulacrum of presence that falsified space and made it into a place of error. Perhaps I should have struggled harder so that he would distance himself more, more sincerely, in a way that was not a piece of trickery, an imposture, the game of understanding and the gaiety of solitude. But for that, didn't he have to be a little more present? Hadn't he said that to me himself? Hadn't he, at a singularly dramatic moment, mentioned the desire to bind me in order to be able to unbind me? Yes, he had revealed himself to me in that thought, and I was still suffering its touch, its glamor.

"When you say 'we,' I'm not sure of what you're saying. It doesn't refer either to you or to me, does it?"

"To us!"

Yes, that created an extraordinary opening, which allowed me to say to him:

"I've been doing a lot of thinking lately. I have the impression that you used to remain more hidden. You were perhaps something extraordinary, but I lived with an extraordinary thing without being disturbed by it, without seeing it and without knowing it."

"Do you miss those days?"

"No, I don't miss them."

"An extraordinary thing."

From the way he repeated it, I thought he had not really heard the word. I had noticed that he liked facts, he had a strange curiosity, almost a passion for the simplest events and things, which he carried off "to his side of things" with a surprising, painful voracity, for often I had the impression that he didn't know what was involved, that the words which designated these things remained opaque for him, at least inasmuch as he had not rolled them around inside his sphere for very long. Nevertheless, I must not have spoken entirely for myself, because he continued to attack me on this word:

"Is it as extraordinary as all that?"

I stood firm:

"Yes, it was, extraordinarily so."

He remained silent before saying to me:

"Aren't you using that word just to be agreeable?"

"To give you an idea of what I think."

"Maybe it's not agreeable to me. Are we so extraordinary for each other?"

"Maybe I'm shielding myself behind that word. It must remind me of certain things. I also find it strange, sometimes, to converse with you."

"Yes, we are conversing."

I was struck, as I had been once before, by how that word seemed to open up, reveal a fissure, whence rose a painful silence, a neutral expanse which he was tempted to travel endlessly, without regard to time, adding one step to another, without hoping ever to encounter fatigue there, exhaustion: this stood between us, and now that I was returning, after a respite—perhaps under the influence of that image—to the room, I saw better—I thought I saw this—how it merged with its own resemblance, which did not surprise me, but prevented me from grasping it in all its extent, also took away my desire to do that, and what struck me even more was how that presence—slipping and yet preserved within that slipping—was of an ambiguous, strange truth, quite indifferent to all truth, to a certainty on the basis of which I could have roamed through it, closed it on its limits. Even if I could try to believe I was responsible for what happened here, this responsibility only marked the emptiness of the event, the lack of seriousness expressed by "Why are you laughing?," a laugh that I would no doubt have remembered hearing, if it had not been the very scattering of that recollection, a light, colorless laugh, around which it was not possible to fix even an invisible presence. I think I had never felt to such a degree how much I, too, stood between us. I had always suspected that when I said "me" it was to oblige him in his turn to say "I," to come out of that depth, that sordid, sterile neutrality where, in order to be on an equal footing, I would have had to become him for myself. A region I had perhaps approached in an earlier time, without realizing it, so much was I joined to him by the movement of youth and liveliness of heart, and I must have had the thought that I believed I was close enough to say "you" to him and far enough away to hear him say "me," that, under the veil of these first persons, shielded by that equality that I had to wrest from him each time by a vehement insistence, I thought, at least momentarily, that I was preserved from the danger of hearing the anonymous, the nameless, speak in him, I must have had that thought, but now I felt it had led me where I wanted to avoid going, for I had perhaps succeeded—by certain ruses—in keeping him shielded from me, but now this contact with me was anonymous, and what resulted from it was nothing other than the lightness of a chattering without truth, the infinite shimmering of joyful reflections and sparkling instants. Nothing extraordinary, as he had said, nothing grave or overwhelming, even though it was impossible to breathe here and dwell here, as though one could only breathe, hope, by means of a little seriousness. This was no doubt why I had to ask him more and more often:

"Can I reflect on it?"—to which he did not fail to answer: "Yes, of course, but for how long?"

When had all this begun? It went on, it did not begin. It did not go on, it was necessarily endless. Why, whatever point I started from, did I necessarily arrive at the same place, the place where I was? And the place where I was, I had to think, was, when we were conversing, the place where he was maintaining his reserve. This reserve was our common space, a "Help yourself yourself," where an unlimited confidence was affirmed that I sometimes thought was reciprocal, but that, for my part, I'm afraid, still hid a desire, the concern to preserve the moment in which we would speak in earnest.

In that space, it was perhaps because I was still trying to hold on to my part—and this was why I was not at the end of my strength, for my part I was not—that I lived in a constant concealment, without knowing where it came from. The simplest thing was to believe that in fact I was concealing something from him, it was easy, he didn't impose himself, he didn't force me in any way. But actually I knew very well that this couldn't be called concealing, and on the contrary, the more I committed myself unreservedly to this space, the more I suffocated at the approach of concealment. He wasn't in the least concerned about what I might think or do. Once, I had been able to live in the world, it didn't bother me and I didn't bother it. But little by little and under the constraint of this concealment, in order to avoid this suffocating element, that I thought I could dissipate this way, I had withdrawn from everything in order not to appear to hide anything from him anymore, so that now, I no longer lived in the world, but in concealment. I tried, behind the shield of this word, to move father forward. I tried to understand why, in this space, there were still knots and tensions, strong areas in which everything was a demand, others in which everything leveled out, an interlacing of expectation and forgetting that incited one to an uninterrupted agitation. I couldn't get rid of the idea that if I had only struggled harder against certain of his remarks, if, instead of hearing them, taking an interest in them, answering them, I had stoutly laid hold of them, by allowing them to mask out, to follow their own path even to the depth of a slow maelstrom, I would have ceased to wander on the surface this way, in a world of vestiges and half-hopes. Still, this was only an idea. At other times, perhaps when I brought a little composure to my reflection, it was my own words that I was prepared to trust. I didn't mean that they intended what I didn't intend, nor even that their capacity, their loyalty were sufficient; on the contrary, they were heavy, not very malleable, and at the same time immoderate, pedantic, loquacious, but it sometimes happened, and, precisely at the approach of concealment, that they appeared to reflect what was essential, respond to it, and what they had said was perhaps insignificant, didn't help me in any way, rather hindered me by allowing me to believe that it had been conversed in emptiness, but only because I obstinately kept myself at a distance; fear, attachment, lack of strength, forgetfulness—this was what kept me withdrawn, whereas speeches, no longer obedient, for some time now, to these general feelings, echoed what was no doubt only an echo, but in this way took their places next to concealment, occupied its place, took its place.

I tried to offer him this remark. I sensed that I should not have done it. It sometimes occurred to me that what he was expecting from me was a tranquil conversation without gaps, a chatty exchange in the center of which he would have dozed like a slight suspicion. But I could not help saying to him:

"Where we are, everything conceals itself, doesn't it?"

Scarcely was it spoken before this remark sank into the emptiness, reverberated there emptily, awoke the infinitely distended outside, the infinite pain of the affirmation occupying all of space, where what was said kept passing through the same point again, was the same, and, always, at whatever moment, said the same thing and eternally remained lacking. I can't say that in this way I was freed of that speech. On the contrary, it returned to me constantly, as though it were its own answer, and each time I was done with it, but each time I expressed it again, for it demanded that: to be said and said again.

I must have stayed in the same place for quite a long time. From one moment to the next, I said to myself: now, it will no longer be possible for me to reflect (when I reflected, I did not reflect, properly speaking, it was like a prayer addressed to time, asking it please to do its work). I was standing a few feet away from a vast, excessively wide bed: I was not even sure, in fact, that it was not the ground, and this prevented me from lying down on it, as I would have liked. I did not see objects distinctly, I perceived the room as a whole, I touched it, as it touched me, through the slight relation that caused the scattering of a slight but infinite laugh to pass between us. This laugh ran along the border of space, without crossing it, but also seemed to be that space, and this gaiety, though foreign to me, nevertheless passed by where I thought I was, dispersed me, dispersed my decision about the serious things I nevertheless had to do. I must have headed toward the kitchen. The thought that for a very long time now I had been heading toward that spot, a thought which itself had a stifling aspect and an amusing aspect, though one kept passing into the other, caused it to happen that when I touched a door, recalling that the storeroom where I was in danger of falling was not far from there, I turned away, and what immediately seized me again was the desire to drink, I was thirsty, that thirst led me back the way I had come.

"Give me a glass of water," I said in a low voice. I could barely hear the words. Yet he answered distinctly:

"I can't give it to you. You know I can't do anything."

I listened to that. The words had something extraordinarily attractive about them, they were distinct, accurate—within my reach—and yet it seemed they didn't know me and I, too, didn't know them. Here was a new phenomenon which, I said to myself, I should worry about for the future, but at that moment it was so light, so irresponsible, and at the same time of such amplitude that I couldn't concern myself about controlling it. Perhaps I didn't understand anything, perhaps I was calling "speech" something that was speechless, but here, what was speechless was already a speech, what was not understood was expressed. I should have gone farther, but I realized I was immobilized by sadness, it was so empty; it spoke in the name of a distance so exhausted, so stubborn, it was bound up with such a pain, a pain so obliterated. Was it here?

I didn't expect an answer, but the one that came was in fact the revelation of the danger in which I found myself. As though the word "here" had drawn me elsewhere or as though I myself, because of my inconstancy, had lightly pushed it before me, I passed back over his words, or, in them, as in a healthy core, still visible, I rediscovered my own, that phrase I had had to say, I rediscovered it, but then I perceived the infinitesimal, frightfully slender bond that connected me to it, its strange, impersonal nature, the infinitesimal part of it that allowed me to say it was mine and consequently say it: when I spoke, didn't I have the impression I was already witnessing that speech from very far away? Didn't I have the feeling that it had preceded me long before, and wasn't it through an unexpected movement, an unexpected withdrawal that, having been face to face with it, I had had the strength not to miss it? Yes, I had had that strength, the strength to prevent it from being said, in my place, by someone or by no one, but if I felt that following that withdrawal I could still have uttered it, I felt no less that, all the same and in any case, it had already uttered itself alone.

What was immediately apparent to me was that I had to remain in that place. Perhaps this discovery did not teach me more than I already knew. Perhaps, by showing me the single point by which I was holding myself to something true, it only tightened around me the anxiety of the emptiness, as though, these words being the only ones in which I still dwelled, I had felt them come apart as the last resting place whence I could stop the errant coming and going. Now I understood clearly—it seemed to me I understood—why I had to stay here. But, being here, where was I? Why near him? Why, behind everything I said and everything he answered, was there this remark: "Where we are, everything conceals itself, doesn't it?"—a remark I understood, did not understand, it had no understanding. Everything was extraordinarily calm, but he did not cease to be equal to that calm, and the silence, profound though it was, was still less silent than he, and constantly appeared to be pursued, obliterated; I could only say to myself: now, that's it for the silence. An impression in which I could not find myself again.

It was a little farther on that I found myself again. I must have been closer to the middle of the room, for it appeared to me in a new light: it was rather low, less broad than long, yet quite large. What stopped me from describing it, from maintaining it firmly in a description, was that I couldn't grasp it. It wasn't a question of remembering, and wasn't I really there, wasn't I in it, really, as he had suggested to me? I did not refuse to believe it, but my belief also lacked reality, so that I didn't really believe it. That this had to do with my relations with him, with the solitude of that "we" in which I had to hold myself, always distancing him so that, in that distance, he could express himself and I could understand him, in which I had to hold myself, but not withdraw: offer myself dangerously to that suffocating element that, when it showed itself, stopped me from concealing myself in it, forced me to wander or dispersed me by holding me open to the power of concealment—this was what I thought; and if I did not understand this thought, at least I rested on it, it was this place, in a certain way, and it was from here that I saw the room where I nevertheless remained. As I looked out through the large bay windows—everything was extraordinarily calm at that moment—and while I saw a strange, dreamy daylight circulate around the curtain of green leaves, a daylight as luminous as I could have imagined, but with a light that was not entirely light, that resembled it, expressed the pleasure of having broken out of the depths to lose itself in the light slipping of the surface, I couldn't help remembering: someone was standing beyond the windows; as soon as I recalled this, he turned toward the window and, without stopping where I was, stared rapidly, with an intense, rapid gaze, at the entire extent, the entire depth of the room. This view vanished almost immediately, but the impression did not vanish, the terrible impression of a return to the same sterile point, at the same indefatigable instant, as though all paths led me back to it, all words at a certain moment passed through this presence whose intensity, whose living force, evoked only the impurity of that moment, the desire in me to find something more to see, to stop there and rest there. This feeling was so strong, so greatly deprived me of the use of myself, that when I heard the murmured words—"Someone is looking at us through the window"; "Through the window?"—I was in some sense delivered, traversed by something happy, and not only because I had yielded to the inevitable, but at that instant something opaque in the word "window" became transparent to me, and what I grasped in

53

that transparency was precisely this light: the moment was approaching when he would no longer understand my words. A presentiment I could not follow through to its end, I lacked the strength, I lacked myself.

I can imagine how long that lasted, for the thought that I had, as I recovered myself, was no doubt the same one I had had as I fell: that, in fact, I was at last falling. But I saw that I had only sat down close to a table, and at the same time I heard the question—it passed through space like an avid shiver—"Are you writing? Are you writing at this moment?" Hearing this, I shivered in turn, I understood that what had awakened me, led me back here, was this voracious murmur that I had not ceased to listen to, for it seemed difficult to escape such an avid continuity, such an uninterrupted insistence, or to set limits to it. It was slightly nauseating, but not without a character of gaiety that invited me to join in with it. Still, I felt a disturbance, an uneasiness that gave me the idea that these words embarrassed me because they followed one another so lightly that I couldn't know if what was involved was a question or only an order, an encouragement. Since I had the impression that these words were not addressed precisely to me, I felt a certain freedom in relation to them, the freedom of being able to answer them lightly myself, if need be. It was this freedom, the impression that I was not being challenged which, without my knowing it, must have driven me to take part. I asked weakly:

"Am I writing?"

This slipped out of me more like a sigh than a speech, but weak as this perturbation was, it was enough to disrupt the equilibrium, and right away, as though attracted by this emptiness, his uninterrupted murmur, which had until now wandered at random, turned around impetuously against me, confronted me, while he asked me with an authority that contrasted ridiculously with the weakness of my resources:

"Are you writing, are you writing at this moment?"

To which I could not help answering him:

"But you know very well that I can no longer write and I am almost not myself any longer."

Words I regretted because of their seriousness, and they were immediately followed, in the furtive manner of a light laugh, though from a little farther away, by his own words:

"Are you writing, are you writing at this moment?"

I didn't allow myself to be deflected from the certainty of being at a turning point that required all my strength, all my attention, by the recollection that I had already, and at almost every instant, been certain I was approaching a turning point from which I then saw that he had only turned me back, led me back. I fully realized where this new assurance came from, this resolution to go farther, yes, in this direction, never in another, a resolution I made at that instant. I could see him: we had stood face to face; at least, I had had this feeling, and before now I had never had it. The fact that nothing happy had resulted from it, that nothing had even resulted at all , wasn't enough to stop me. For this feeling—not the feeling of having my back to the wall, but the desire, faced with this formidable demand that had looked at me, stared at me where I was not dwelling, trying to draw me along into the emptiness of an airless and rootless time—was the desire, faced with such a demand, to come back to something true which, in order to answer him, had spoken in me. Even if he had disregarded this answer, it had still entered his space, I was now establishing myself on it, I had reached it, I had to maintain it even in the midst of the regret from which I also could not entirely separate myself.

This was so much the case that, thinking of what he had often said to me—"Well, another day has passed, hasn't it?"—I welcomed this remark with satisfaction, with gratitude, as though from time immemorial he had been destined to show me this new day. Yes, the old day had passed, and the glow that was illuminating this moment was like that which might have succeeded in announcing to me: "This is the point you have reached, this is what you are." I was still close to the table. I was no less close to the decisive quality of my remark, near which I remained, yet without being able to distinguish them from his, from what I was certainly obliged, if only because I had answered him, to consider to be his question. The question had not been shaken by it, but that only rendered more significant a fact I was gradually becoming aware of: that it had brought my answer with it and that now I scarcely recognized the latter as mine, mingled as it was with that murmur which remained, in the distance, like a promise and a seduction. I considered the thing, at first with the enthusiasm of my confidence in that moment, but gradually with the foreboding, the apprehension, of having pointlessly handed over to him the center of myself, the heart of the citadel—far from having won it away from him—and when he said to me: "But isn't that what writing is?" I did not in the least experience the pleasure, the interest, of a new remark, but a spasm of disgust at rediscovering our two sentences clasped against each other, mingled in a cold intimacy, in the emptiness of their own indifference, and it was as though I had had to fight far away from myself, but also far away from him, where we were neither one nor the other.

It was at this distance, from very far away, that I heard him repeat softly: "I think that's what writing is," no doubt to let me know that if he was recovering the advantage, it was not in an underhand way, but by complying with the truth, by welcoming it more deeply than I, at a depth before which I stopped short. I, too, was tempted to descend to this depth, but I could do no more than reaffirm myself:

"Even where I am with it? At the point where I am with it?"—the purpose of which was mainly to ask him where I was. I expected to hear him answer me by echoing me: "But where are you with it?" and perhaps this remark would have opened a path for me toward myself, but since he said nothing more, I wasn't in control of the silence, I couldn't resist this murmur, which underlay it. I asked him:

"We're connected by writings, aren't we?"

To which he immediately answered: "Yes, that's right," and then added the following, which showed me that he did not forget anything, that nothing was lost:

"But you know there must be no name between us."

I hardly took any notice of this last remark, perhaps because in myself I was no longer back at that moment when I wanted to give him a name, or perhaps because, without my knowing it, starting at that moment, I had lent him one. But above all, I was distanced from this thought by another thought: we were connected, he had recognized this, he had recognized it by a "Yes" of which I grasped the immensity, the immutable, immobile force that also confirmed all our past words, but in which above all reverberated the affirmation of the whole space we had entered, that space from which there was nothing to cut back, nothing to push back, which, even in the emptiness, affirmed, and affirmed again, in such a way that it seemed to warn me that henceforth, whatever might be my refusals, my statements that "I can't do anymore," everything would nevertheless be resumed by that monumental "Yes," everything would end in it slowly, solemnly. "Yes, that's right." A calm expanse, yet one I couldn't remain close to; on the contrary, what occurred to me was that I should make use of it and that since we were connected, we were connected starting now and for now. Now, as he had promised me, he was going to "do something for me." I asked him:

"Don't you want to help me now?"

It seemed to me he hesitated, with an infinite hesitation that I filled with the firmness, the exigency of my expectation, of my impatience, too, which closed again when he answered me, from very far away, in a low voice:

"You know I can't help you."

I immediately stood up and, as though my thirst had returned, went to the kitchen. There, I looked for a glass, but, for a reason I could not discern, that search came to nothing or something caused me not to go on with it. Coming back to the room, where I was surprised by the darkness, I heard him ask:

"What have you just been doing? Are you in pain?"

"I'm tired, but I feel better already."

"Yes, you'll get your strength back."

Because I was bothered by how little light there was, I said to him:

"I haven't yet spoken with you about this, but very near here there's a large bed, and I'm going to lie down on it."

"A large bed?"

At that moment, I searched my mind to find out whether I had really drunk that glass of water just now. Soon I was almost sure that it had not happened, something had stopped me from doing it. I reflected a little more. Finally, I said to him:

"I've forgotten something, I must go back to the kitchen."

"As you like," he said. "You have plenty of time."

Yet I didn't go back. Now I lacked the strength I had thought I owed to the drink. I sat down on the edge of the bed, no doubt in order to continue reflecting, but soon I also lacked the strength to think all this was important. I only asked myself if someone else had been there in my place, which seemed to explain why I retained such a cold memory of that action. I also thought about his last remark, on which I was now invited to rest. I thought about it with friendliness, even though this rest was a sleepless one, an empty one. But I also desired nothing other than that emptiness and that immobility.

Often before, in moments of great anguish, I had dreamed of breaking all ties, it seems to me I had said this to him, it seems to me it was in order to untie these bonds that I had wanted to tie them, to tie myself to him in such a way that the understanding, having become real, could really be destroyed. Perhaps I had even dreamed further; perhaps I only approached in order to fight him, in a combat that would separate him from himself, even if only by separating me from myself forever. A dream that expressed only my lassitude, the sterility of my lassitude, the point of forgetfulness where I was trying in vain to fool myself about what I knew best, and what I knew was that I could not take anything the wrong way, coming from him. In the most unhappy moments, I think I never revealed a single twinge of regret, of resentment, a single feeling of being at fault—which, in return, no doubt deprived me of hope. It doesn't matter. I never failed to say he was right, I who alone was right, and he never caused me to be guilty with respect to myself. If this is what loses me by preventing me from losing myself, if this is what binds me by ceaselessly pushing back the end, I accept this bond and I will endure this trial through the infinity of time.

Why this confidence? And is it confidence? I do not rely more on him than on myself, only a little more on him because he is less sure than I. A little more on him, because I find a little less in him than in me. Confidence? But at least nothing that might summon up distrust, nothing that ought to incline me to regret this encounter, if it took place. Confidence? Then confidence in the abyss, confidence that the abyss won't fail me, won't betray me.

I've never thought he might reveal anything important to me; I don't expect any revelation from him. This, too, makes us right for each other. And yet, didn't I expect something, didn't I want to ask him, as I do still at this moment: "I can trust you, can't I?"—and I immediately hear him answer me:

"Yes, but on condition that I can trust you."

"You mean I have to talk to you incessantly, without stopping?"

"Talk, describe things."

Which was enough to awaken a spirit of uncertainty.

"Why describe?" I asked him. "There's nothing to describe, there's almost nothing left."

Why this voracious hunger for facts that he perhaps didn't understand but that he wanted to have anyway, this blind hunger in him that I immediately felt in myself as the uneasiness of nausea? Was he really looking for something? But he wasn't looking for anything, he couldn't be looking for anything in particular; to believe that would have driven me mad on the spot, and I didn't even think he had a particular relationship with me: not with me, not with me. And yet, I felt the approach of this aimless, patient voracity, that awaited, without ever becoming discouraged, an infinitesimal particle of an insignificant reality—in the form of my own disgust I felt its approach, its groping search, which I had to stop, at least, if not satisfy. What could I give him? A gesture, another step, a sigh, a last sigh? Or his own words, which I would have liked to keep at a distance once and for all, but which he tirelessly seized again, as though in them there was still a vestige of life which he wanted to reduce even more in order to disappropriate me of it, so that I would have nothing left that belonged to me? I said to him with a brusqueness that tore even me apart:

"You want to know where I am? But nothing has changed, we're still in the same spot, we'll always be here; yes, I find it strange to converse with you, strange to come to this, strange to stay here; why does it cost me so much strength? Why must I devote myself to something that costs me so much, without respite, without wanting it, without expecting anything from it? Am I going to continue chatting with you? It exhausts me, it doesn't even exhaust me."

So many words that expressed only the dangerous increase in my strength, as I immediately became aware, and much more so, even, when I heard him ask me:

"You want to see something new?" as though he himself, curiously, was infinitely avid for what might be new. This movement caused my agitation to subside, obliged me to return silently to the truth of that moment:

"Not necessarily new; perhaps nothing that would be new for anyone."

I imagined he was ready to elaborate on this theme, but soon he, in turn, cut it short:

"No, nothing new."

A remark in which I had to steep myself. It was in relation to this remark that I said to him a little later:

"At this moment, I am sitting on the edge of a bed, I will no doubt get up, soon it will be day."

"It's dark, isn't it?"

"It's not very dark, it's the light that's dark."

"Don't you want to stretch out now?"

"Yes, I think I'm going to stretch out, it's a large bed, unmade and disorderly. Do you want me to describe things to you as I see them?"

"Yes, that's it, as we are able to see them, as we will see them."

Nevertheless, I did not lie down. I had in some sense forgotten what was needed in order to do that, and yet, lying down, I would no doubt have been closer to that shared vision into which he was drawing me in defiance of my strength or so as to turn me away from it, destroy it by ignoring it. If I had stretched out, what would have happened? I could at least imagine: nothing was more tempting than that great stretch of space, already uncovered, that immensity where there would have been no respect for my person, where my rest would not be merely like a companion asleep near me in my wakefulness. Why not try it? I dream of that a few moments. During this dream, my hand is somehow invited by the tranquillity of the space, there nothing moves, nothing stable or moving, but a smooth immobility toward which I turn as I lie down on my side, which does not disturb or restrict the expanse of space. It is true that I am only on the edge of the real posture which I recognize a little beyond me in the form of a slight stirring which I feel, with a certain surprise, as a firm, almost solid resistance. Here there is something like a single wrinkle of space, I see it, in some way, and the fact that it should be just there, like a

61

discordant irregularity, ought to warn me, but already unconcerned, I tip myself back lightly, joyously, trusting in space, in its indifference and its inattention. Thus, this latter movement is accomplished with a facility that expresses my own cheerfulness, but scarcely does it assert itself than all the power of the emptiness tightens around me, encloses me, holds me back and pushes me back into the depth of an endless fall, so that the gap into which I fall has the exact dimensions of my body, is my body into which I can't possibly fall and against which I collide at this moment as against a cold, foreign presence that throws me back where I am. This is the beginning, I said to myself, things began this way. Yes, such is the dream, and I have a suspicion of what it would like to show me: that if it is now forbidden for me to stretch out, this is because I am already stretched out at that point where, nevertheless, I am no longer there, but someone is there. What does such a moment want from me? It takes all my strength away from me, it leaves me here, not standing, not lying down, without rights and without repose, not working and yet occupied without respite by this idleness, not ignorant but knowing too much, not immobile but on the edge of an eternal agitation. What does it ask me to do? The fall is endless, it therefore leaves me nothing to do, I can't stop the fall, I don't have the means to do it, I'm not even falling, I'm only sitting on the edge of a bed, while there plunges into the distance the slight derision of a murmur: "Are you writing, are you writing at this moment?"

I can't say I tore myself from such a dream. It's true that in this night—I call it night, and yet it is the brilliant light of summer—I am still bound to a certain effort, to a life that has the appearance of life. I sometimes hear myself thinking: this is perhaps only the beginning. I sometimes also believe that even though nothing is happening, I am drawing near the place where I was hoping to fight. It was here, over there, where I heard him talking from, and it was the fight that was talking to me. Here the decisive fight takes place, everything

62

is ready for the decision, the words themselves are ready, they are even already spoken, the decision is not only ready, it has been made, has everything therefore come to an end? Yes, everything has come to an end; and what was decided? Just this—that there would be no end, so that I continue to hear the fight, I approach the spot where the decision was made, and I say to myself: perhaps this is still merely the beginning, always merely the beginning.

I don't think about the future, I don't give myself a future, and not even a present. The present keeps bending, traversed by that empty gaiety that is only the limitless and empty absence of all present, it does not see itself in the past, nothing in it passes, nothing finishes, and if it becomes so heavy for me to carry, it is because of this burden of lightness, this laughing load I have to hold up in the center of a dreamy day that hides me from myself. It is in such a day that I must decide if he is really inviting me to write. He does not force me to do it, he does not even advise me to do it. But nevertheless, he has put into my mind the thought that if we are bound together, we are bound by writings. This means that I am in control of the reality of this bond; to make this bond real, I must therefore write, and not once and for all, but all the time, or perhaps one single time, this is not specified, but a time for which I have plenty of time, a time that exhausts all the reality of time. A tempting thought, no doubt empty like a dream, oppressive and nauseating like everything that is empty, but in the middle of which I can dwell all the more lightly because it does not ask either realization or even the dream of that realization.

If he were tempting me only with that thought, I would be able to resist it easily, it would exhaust itself, dissolved within the space that brings it to me. No, he doesn't invite me to write, he doesn't ask it of me, but he seeks to persuade me that I am not doing anything else. And how can I avoid that impression? Against it, I have no defense, it has something necessary about it that goes beyond the conciliatory tranquillity of dreams, it has no need of proofs, it can't be overcome by anything, it collides, as against itself, against the truth of appearance that shows me sitting on the edge of the bed or not sitting, but perhaps lying down, or not even lying down, incapable of doing anything but wandering. I can't refute it, because it leaves me no room in which to move around it, it occupies all of space, it is tied to the affirmation of all of space, it affirms absolutely, and I can't think of breaking this circle, I don't think of it because I belong to this circle, and it is possible, in fact, that I'm not writing, because I can't, and I am almost no longer myself, but that's what it is, to write: at the point where I am, nothing else can be expressed, and this emptiness, this immobility is nothing more, and I can't do, I don't want, anything else.

What makes this situation terrible is that despite everything it demands infinitely, not of me, perhaps, or this demand demands this: that I not be taken into account. It does not consider my resources, these are perhaps very paltry, they are perhaps relatively still infinite, in any case obviously insufficient. Nevertheless, something is asked of me, it is not a duty, nor an order—this is not asked of me, it must be accomplished by the fact that I have come to this, and to have come to this means: to go further, further in this direction, never in another.

I must say it, since I am here to say it: it is a frightening ordeal. It has no limits, it knows neither day nor night, it concerns itself with neither events nor desires; what is possible, it pushes away; what cannot be, that alone satisfies it; of him who has nothing it asks; he who answers its demand doesn't know it and, because of that, doesn't answer. It may be that at one time I thoughtlessly obeyed its call, but then who doesn't obey? he who is not called? but obeying proves nothing about the call, the call always takes place, it doesn't need anyone to answer, it never really takes place, that is why it isn't possible to answer it. But he who does not answer, more than any other, is enclosed in his answer.

When did I give myself up to this risk? Perhaps while sleeping, perhaps in the course of a night when, by an unreflecting movement, by a single word into which I had put all of myself, the decision of time, having been shaken, caused me to pass into the indecision of the absence of time, there where the end is always still the unending. But if that is an imprudence, why mightn't I have committed it? could I live without committing it? did I regret it? Free not to surrender myself to this risk, don't I surrender myself to it from one moment to the next? and at present, is this beginning again? but nevertheless it is not beginning again, it is an absolutely different moment, without any parallel, without any tie to the past, without any concern for the future, and yet it is also beginning again, is the same, is the emptiness of repetition, the infinite pain that always passes through the same point again, and always, at whatever moment it may be, this is said, and eternally I express it.

He doesn't rush me, he isn't an adversary, he doesn't oppose me, this is why I can't defend myself by fighting, the fight isn't even deferred, he himself is the incessant deferral of the fight. And in a certain way I am happy about it, because where I am, reserve obliges me to reserve myself, and his infinite complicity lends itself to this, to the point where I not only allow myself to turn away from myself, but am entirely this infinite turning away. When he sought to persuade me that I wasn't doing anything else, I never opposed this movement in any other way than by concessions that I allowed myself to wrest away, that I offered him with the thought that, this way, the moment that had seemed to me to put us face to face would return, it was this moment that I had in view, it was this, I'm sure, that, after having inspired in me a gesture of frankness and firmness, drew me along to a place where there was no longer anything firm. It began when, bringing me back to the phrase that scarcely was one, that in any case left the field open to all the others—"Am I writing?"—it seemed to me he was inviting me to complete it, sustain it, which, at a certain moment, caused me to add:

"Yes, at one time; perhaps, at one time." A miserable remark, miserably defective, in which "perhaps" tried to appease "at one time," whereas "at one time" already contains the uncertainty of a "perhaps" and this certainly showed how weak my "Yes" still was, but also how "at one time" was for me a weak defense against the "Yes" I had said. I saw this even before he repeated: "At one time," and when he had repeated it, I saw it even more from the neutral tone that was his, that asked for no clarification, added nothing to the word, only said what was said by the word, which in this nakedness only appeared all the more suspect, deceptive, inconsistent, without frankness, not even doubtful, but having no other form than its own doubt, entirely traversed and formed by the cloud of this doubt, in which all that could be seen was my desire to preserve the present moment. A little after, he asked: "And what were you writing?"—to which, seeing his insistence and in order to try to take back what I had granted to him, I answered:

"Perhaps it wasn't me, but someone else, someone who is merely close to me."

A point of view he immediately adopted:

"Well, then, what was he writing?"

I listen to this. Who is he addressing? who is involved here? who is speaking? who is listening? who could answer such a distance? this comes from so far away and it doesn't even come, why is he ignoring me? why is this ignorance within my reach? why does it make itself understood? A speech? And yet not a speech, barely a murmur, barely a shiver, less than silence, less than the abyss of emptiness: the fullness of emptiness, something one can't silence, occupying all of space, uninterrupted and incessant, a shiver and already a murmur, not a murmur, but a speech, and not just any speech, but distinct, appropriate: within my reach. I summoned up my whole being to answer him:

"He wasn't writing, and he mustn't be involved here."

But as though he had heard only the beginning of my answer or as though my remark itself had wiped out the prohibition against speaking, he asked: "And at present, is he writing?"—which was immediately followed by the slight derision of his words: "Are you writing, are you writing at this moment?"

What is going to happen, then? Did I really have this desire to steal away, to unload myself on someone else? or rather to conceal in me the unknown, not to disturb it, to wipe out its footsteps so that what it has accomplished may be accomplished without leaving any remains, in such a way that it not be accomplished for me who dwells on the edge, outside the event, which no doubt passes by with the brilliance, noise, and dignity of lightning, without my being able to do more than perpetuate its approach, take its indecision by surprise, maintain it, maintain myself in it without yielding. Was this at an earlier time, where I lived and worked, in the little room in the form of a watchtower, in that place where already, in some sense having disappeared, far from feeling unburdened of myself, I had, on the contrary, the duty to protect that disappearance, to persevere in it in order to push it farther, always farther? Wasn't it there, in the extreme distress that is not even someone's distress, that I had been presented with the right to speak of myself in the third person? Didn't I have to keep the secret concerning "him" even from my companion, even without knowing if I would have the strength, if the secret did not signify lack of strength, withdrawal, the emptiness of the moment? Didn't I have my attention constantly turned to him? I don't mean I was thinking about him: he couldn't have tolerated a thought, he had nothing in him that could have allowed itself to be thought, but surely I would have liked to convince myself that my task was to protect him against the nameless, to keep the nameless by my side and not give anything over to him but myself. A thought that pleased me, because it assigned me a role and gave me a certain importance, but I nevertheless had enough sense to reject it, for how was I to defend him, I who didn't know him, and from whom would he have had to protect himself, if not from me? What was more, I knew that to think of him, to claim to protect him, was only a sly way of revealing him, and I also knew this: unmasked, he could no longer be anything else—but me.

At that moment, this was what I sensed: for a long time now, my companion had been trying to attain it, to look at it in me. I was not intentionally betraying it, but I had become too weak, I was almost no one, and to see me was already to see it, to speak to me was no longer to speak of me. What is going to happen, then? Why try to stop it?

I think I have to write. I think all the words we have exchanged are crowded around me and I won't resist their pressure for very long, that probably for a long time now, an infinite time, I haven't really been resisting them any longer. It seems to me that if I write, it will be I writing: I will bind my companion to me in such a way that he will approach only me and that what must remain unknown will remain safeguarded. In this way, the space opened by his allusion will close again. In this fissure there is a danger that I don't fully understand, a danger that is not merely mortal, but rather holds death in check, is perhaps death, but held in check. And at the same time, wasn't it strangely attractive? didn't it make what he said firmer, more true, indifferent and true? didn't a whistle pass through that fissure that called to mind the wind of the distance, the freshness of the natural air, and no doubt I had only received it exhausted, more a memory than the force of the wind, but if the fissure had been enlarged, perhaps the open air itself would have seized me and carried me along, perhaps it would have been there that, if I threw out my anchor, instead of hearing it scrape my empty depth of myself, I would rediscover the deeps of the open sea, and not infinity, for which I have no need, but the single moment in which I would tie myself to the end with enough strength for it to become true, for it not to be excluded from the truth and for the truth to light up in it.

An impression that was powerful, pressing, that forced me to go back to the distant period, when I still heard the sound of the wind shaking the house during the autumn storms, to ask myself if, should I truly come to the point of writing, I wouldn't need to be helped in my task by that work and that effort of the wind, and I asked myself why, for so long now, I had been kept away from that help, dwelling in such a calm that I probably wouldn't have had the strength to tolerate even a slight whistle finding its way through the vent, yet I wasn't surprised by this, and if the wind, with the gusts of approaching winter, seemed driven far back by a force infinitely greater than its own, I said to myself that I knew this force and that it was the power of the memory of summer.

In any case, I couldn't assign an exact moment to the answer I would give him, if I ever succeeded in saying to him:

"Yes, at this moment, exactly at this moment." That these last words were the only ones that counted in his sentence was what I discovered with a sort of gratitude, so that this whole sentence, so anguishing for me, regained a youthful face from this, and he himself a more truthful presence. As I reflected on it from this new perspective, I saw that it was an almost innocent murmur, something a little more disturbing than the sound of blood or the beating of an agitated heart, but that circulated through the house joyfully, without respite. If I no longer heard it, I imagined it had gone to another spot, had been called elsewhere by its own gaiety, by the lightness that turned it into a question. Sometimes—and then a certain uneasiness returned—I asked myself if that appearance of caprice, of restless and aimless vagabondage did not conceal a search, an obscure hunt, a stubborn pursuit,

and this feeling, though I did not believe it, became an un-
controllable alarm, when it seemed to me that it was approaching a spot I could have situated, for instance the staircase, or that it was flying up and assaulting the little room,
the place where I had the impression I had already returned
once with my companion. Terrible imprudence. But I must
say that just as I had enough confidence in him, in his loyalty, to be assured that he would not play his game alone,
even though he was capable of coming to me by unprepared
paths, to the same degree I mistrusted certain of his words
which I did not distinguish, once they were said, from mine,
a mistrust that yielded to a joyful enthusiasm once I recognized their frivolity, their fussiness and futility, but which
weighed most of the time with a heavy weight on me, with
the weight formed of their own heaviness, their inertia and,
coupled with their irresponsibility, the perseverance that made
them sterile, unreal and eternal. They sustained a certain life
in this house from which I was not very willing to turn
away—another source of their danger—a life that held me in
a place, where I should not have lingered, and I sometimes
asked myself if, in these other rooms where no doubt, because of them, I would stay at certain times, I did not live
with a life that was more alert, more carefree, and on terms
of equality with the earth. As I heard them talk in that joyful,
incessant way, it would only have required of me an effort
against myself, a momentary forgetting of the truth, to let
myself believe I was talking with beings much more real
than I was myself, just then, at least more alive, yes, beings,
here, from whom I was only separated because I was not
here, or if I was here, I was surrounded by the solitude of
that "we are alone" that had opposed me, every time I moved
away from myself.

In these moments then, it was the need to pacify those
words, suspend for a moment their agitated flight through
the house, bring them back, also, to themselves by keeping
them away from the feverish earth, that obliged me to ask

myself if I shouldn't write—now. It seemed to me that only by writing could I soothe this uneasiness, which, it seemed, could carry them to meet a mouth that was alive, capable of giving them the happiness of breath, and that I could also, in this uneasiness, soothe the image which, at their summons, was crossing through the days and nights. A task concerning which I barely glimpsed what it demanded of me, for I no doubt found it easy to wish to calm the moment, free it of the distress that was making it appear, but if I could hope to succeed in this by bringing the words back to their birthplace, I myself would perhaps have to descend, into another time, pass into a place where it would no longer be a question if appearance or image, but a supreme moment toward which I would have to descend firmly and which I would not be able to seize except by desiring it with all the strength and transport of passion.

In this way I understood better why this was what it was, to write: I understood it, I mean this word became completely other, much more demanding even than I had thought it was. To be sure, it was not to my power that it had made its appeal, nor to myself either, but to "this moment" when I could do nothing—and thus it seemed to me that writing had to consist in drawing near that moment, would not give me power over it, but, by some act unknown to me, would make me a gift of this moment, near which, for an infinite time now, I had dwelled without reaching it—far from here and yet here. I clearly perceived the risk I was going to expose myself to: instead of making the words go back over the frontier they had crossed, the risk, on the contrary, of disturbing them more and more, of tormenting them by driving them mad with an empty, unbridled desire, to the point that, at a certain moment, passing through me in their frantic pursuit, they would carry me once again toward a space dangerously open to the illusion of a world to which we would, however, not have access, for the thought that this access might be granted to us, if the assault was conducted

71

with enough vehemence and skill, had not yet come to tempt me, that temptation was only part of the risk, the risk was the pivot around which what was threat turned immediately into hope, and I myself turned around myself, given up to every appeal of this place where all I could do was wander.

To say that I understand these words would not be to explain to myself the dangerous peculiarity of my relations with them. Do I understand them? I do not understand them, properly speaking, and they too who partake of the depth of concealment remain without understanding. But they don't need that understanding in order to be uttered, they do not speak, they are not interior, they are, on the contrary, without intimacy, being altogether outside, and what they designate engages me in this "outside" of all speech, apparently more secret and more interior than the speech of the innermost heart, but, here, the outside is empty, the secret is without depth, what is repeated is the emptiness of repetition, it doesn't speak and yet it has always been said already. I couldn't compare them to an echo, or rather, in this place, the echo repeated in advance: it was prophetic in the absence of time.

The fact that they were deprived of intimacy to this degree was, it seems to me, what associated me, in the course of their wandering, their coming and going, with a feeling of infinite unhappiness, with the chill of the greatest distress I had ever had to endure, a distress that immediately reverberated in an endless gaiety that made him ask me: "Why are you laughing?"—which I could not answer except to say:

"Because I'm not alone," a phrase that, in its turn, flew off dangerously through the house. Perhaps the idea that I must save them from this lack of intimacy also belongs to the project of writing, an idea I could have had at an earlier time, an idea to which, no doubt uselessly, I sacrificed my right to summon another person and say "you" to him. But this is only an idea from an earlier time, I can't hope to give them what I myself have been deprived of, I don't even want to, they often please me extraordinarily this way (which is another aspect of the danger): they beguile me by this busy lack of work, this torment which is a kind of laughter, this presence in which I am never "me" for them nor they "you" for me, a presence that is no doubt disabling, for I'm not able to deal with anything in them, disabling but attractive, an enigma there is no need to elucidate, the key word to the enigma is this enigma, capable not of devouring me, but of associating me with its devouring avidity.

If I question myself seriously, I must recognize that, if not all these words, at least the most brilliant and the most enticing, the ones that uplift me almost outside of myself (and in a certain light each is always the most brilliant), could only steal away or oppose "this moment" in which I ought to write. And I recognize it with all the more apprehension because they sometimes give me the opposite feeling: "sometimes" means during certain periods which, to distinguish them from others in which everything seems easier, I call nocturnal, and they themselves appear to me profoundly nocturnal, it is in these moments that they crowd around me, like dreams being dreamt by my side, and I myself am only an image in their dream, I feel the power of their conjuring and how they, too, feel the strength of my dream, feeling the infinite desire to participate in it, to enter into the sphere of that dream, a desire so lively that it is itself the night, that it creates the night in which we find ourselves together again, reunited, but through the ignorance we have in common, through the community of our ignorance which causes it to happen that even when I hear them, I do not hear them, and when I speak them, nothing is said, even though everything may be said in them forever. And no doubt what they may ask of me has no relation to the idea of writing, it is rather they who want to be inscribed in me as though to allow me to read on myself, as on my gravestone, the word of the end, and it is true that, during these nocturnal moments, I have the feeling of being able to read myself that way, read in a dangerous way, well beyond myself, to the point where I am no longer there, but someone is there.

Beautiful hours, profound words which I would like to belong to, but which would, themselves, also like to belong to me, words empty and without connection. I can't question them and they can't answer me. They only remain close to me, as I remain close to them. That is our dialogue. They stand motionless, as though erect in these rooms; at night, they are the concealment of the night; in the day, they have the transparency of the day. Everywhere I go, they are there.

What do they want? We're not familiar to one another, we don't know one another. Words from the empty depth, who has summoned you? Why have you become manifest to me? Why am I occupied with you? I shouldn't occupy myself with you, you shouldn't occupy yourselves with me, I must go farther, I won't unite you to hope or to the life of a breath.

I don't know that they press on me, but I sense it. I see a sign of it in the immobility which, even when they seem to wander, even when I leave them, keeps them crowded around me in a circle whose center I am in spite of myself. And this circle is sometimes larger, sometimes smaller, but for me the distance doesn't change, and the circle is never interrupted, the expectation is never broken, I could call myself a prisoner of that expectation if it were more real, but since it remains silent and uncertain, I am only a prisoner of the uncertainty of the expectation.

Am I their goal, what they are seeking? I will not believe it. But sometimes they stare at me with a power so restrained, a silence so reserved, that this silence points me out to myself; then I have to remain firm, I have to struggle with my refusal to believe, and the more I struggle, in general successfully, the more I see that I owe the strength that gives me this success only to them, to their proximity, to the firmness of their inattention.

I'm not their goal, but why do they remain? why are they turned toward me, even if they are not directed toward me?

Why, outside my companion and as though to a certain extent they had a free life, must I look at them without linking them to him, with a gaze that is perhaps connected to the word "write," but that is, in that case, connected to it as the thing that may best turn me away from it? I can ask myself that, I could try to find out at what moment they first attracted my gaze, they turned me in their direction to the point that all things are visible to me through their transparent presence and they hold me in the fixedness of their appearance. When did this happen? A vain question, it has always been happening; but I didn't perceive it, which says a good deal about my blindness, I didn't see them as an obstacle, I didn't see them, whereas now, I am looking at them: as though they have risen from their graves.

I didn't invoke them, I am without power over them, and they have no relations with me. We remain side by side, it's true, but I don't know them; I live close to them, and perhaps I must live because of them, perhaps because of them I am sustained in myself, but I am also somehow separated from that proximity, it is in that separation that we are close, there they remain, there they pass, and they respond to no one.

They don't importune, nor do they attract me; if they attracted me, from that assurance I would also draw the strength to drive them back. But I don't desire that, desire can't penetrate this circle, only forgetfulness penetrates it. It seems to me that here forgetfulness does its work, a forgetfulness of a particular sort, in which I don't forget myself, behind which I shield myself, on the contrary, as behind a borrowed "me," one that allows me always to say "me" with a semblance of authority. I forget nothing, it is in this respect that I belong to forgetfulness.

They're always together. No doubt this means I can only see them together, together even though unconnected, motionless around me though wandering. I see them all, never one in particular, never one single one in the familiarity of an undivided gaze, and if, even so, I try to stare at one of them separately, what I'm looking at then is a terrible, impersonal presence, the frightening affirmation of something I don't understand, don't penetrate, that isn't here and that nevertheless conceals itself in the ignorance and emptiness of my own gaze. But this occurs only when I try to isolate one of them, to maintain in a single one of them what makes them all separate, what keeps them all at a distance.

I mustn't alarm them, nor tame them. I must remain still so that they will remain still. Deal with their presence in a loyal way, and "loyally" means without attributing any law to them, without attributing myself to this presence as to a law—and perhaps not taking them into account. But the fact of once having opened my eyes on them prevents me now from ever closing my eyes again. For one instant, this was visible to me, and now it is this instant in which everything is visible to me that I look at and retain, despite myself, without being able to drive it away. In return, and because, in a way I don't understand, I fascinate them, I have to remain within their fascination. This isn't noticed, doesn't disturb appearances, is nothing but an uncertain expectation. Next to them, I am like a man who has already held himself up in the water too long and who sees, coming to meet him, what appears to be the body of a drowned man: only one? perhaps two, perhaps ten, he can't distinguish them, nothing distinguishes them, and they probably do him no harm, they merely hold themselves motionless around him; if he asks himself: What do they want? he knows very well that this question is without meaning, without reality, just as that meeting is not real. Nevertheless, eventually, and because he is growing more and more tired, he can't help finding this immobility heavy, it presses on him, it clings to him, and he asks himself: what does this immobility want?

Everything has an end, but distress does not, it does not know sleep, it does not know death, from one instant to the next I put this to the test; day doesn't illuminate it, night is its depth, its living memory. The circle they form around me encloses me on the outside and yet always within me still. It is infinite, and because of this I suffocate inside it; one can only suffocate in infinity, but I suffocate slowly here, infinitely. I thought I was only the center of this circle, but I already fill it entirely, that is why everything is motionless and, they themselves being crowded against this immobility, I think I see them, but I am really touching them, they hold me against myself, as I hold them desperately beyond me.

The feeling I am left with: I will not yield, I can't do otherwise.

Strange impression of daylight in this feeling, not that of any sort of hope, but of an accurate direction, of confidence that doesn't alter, of affirmation that persists: I will go in that direction, never in another.

A feeling that is immediately disturbed, for the thought goes through me that if I wanted to, I would receive an increase in strength from them. But this is the strength to which I can't consent; why? I don't know more precisely; nevertheless, I still know that this depends on me, on me at each instant, I know it even in forgetfulness and even when, looking at them, I have the presentiment that it would be enough for me to say to one of them—but only to one—"Come," for it to shout its name, and right away I would emerge from that reserve in which, even if the instant doesn't stand there, I stand in its place, in that spot where, in the confidence that is suitable to the abyss, I await the instant that will say to me: "Now everything is all right, you don't have to talk anymore."

Then this other thought: instead of remaining in that reserve, haven't you already abandoned it? have you even touched it? perhaps you've never been outside, or only in an earlier time, but not now, not again, this can't take place again, everything is empty and lifeless.

What darkened, obliterated those hours, I feel, was that the immobility was still only the agitation, the feverishness that came to me from that presence, the strength their proximity communicated to me, the desire that strength gave me to attribute a goal to them, to free them by an intention: did they really want to come alive? did they want to make themselves free, not with a second-hand freedom, but free with respect to their origin and by obliterating it, by forgetting it, with a forgetfulness deeper than death? A terrible thought, a thought in which forgetfulness is at work.

Escape them? With me they escape, I carry them along without even noticing it, or I think I see them wandering once again through the house, but I'm the one continuing to perform the gestures of life. Sometimes—and this should frighten me, but this doesn't frighten me—it seems to me I look at them in a more familiar way. Especially at night, thinking freely of my past life, I have the impression that they're taking part in it, that they're feeding on it, that they could live it, if I thought about it in a more lively way. Then they close me in tightly, and in this irresolute immobility I can only become their dream, the dream of this night in which they remain close to me, as I remain close to them, in the intimacy of this night which ceaselessly passes through the day, which is the day for me, in which they are standing, looming up all around, forming the empty, infinite circle that is still me, even if already I'm no longer there. In these moments, how can I see them as an obstacle? how can I think they interpose themselves between their origin and me? Instead, I trust in them, I look at them in that trustfulness that addresses neither one nor the other, that doesn't attribute a gaze to them, that doesn't discover a face in them, that leaves them what they are, images without eyes, a closed immobility that silently conceals itself and in which concealment is revealed. We're so close it seems to me I form a circle with them, form a circle around someone whom neither they nor I see, for my eyes are no more open than theirs are. This explains our new familiarity, the different air I breathe, the expectation that is not theirs but mine, an expectation of which I am not the prisoner, but the guardian. We stand around him. We don't know if he is one alone or if he is many. We don't know if he is sleeping, riveted to his rest, or if he is coming down to us, without knowing it and without seeing us. Our task is to maintain the circle, but why? We don't know.

From these moments I return preoccupied. In a certain way, this preoccupation prevents my return, it also prevents me from bringing back with me the part of me that belongs to the circle or, if it comes back, it is foreign to me, not an enemy, but distant, as though I had almost nothing more in common with myself. I realized by this sign that, even though I was neither more removed nor more separated from him, it was harder for me to turn toward my companion, perhaps because when I turned toward him, something in me turned away from him, but it was also the opposite: I had to search in vain for a conversation that had been pursued, pushed farther. Formerly, at a period when my unconcern allowed me to find support in things, the thought had come to me to fight him with what was strongest in him: I would raise silent walls around him; I would never question him, and if he passed through the interstices of time I wouldn't answer him. What did I have in view? To control him? to treat him as an equal? Maybe my desire was more obscure, more profoundly tied to him, and this desire is what I recover today, but in the form of a suffocating apprehension, the anxious feeling the word "forgetfulness" brings with it. I think that at certain moments I'm afraid of forgetting him, losing him in forgetfulness and making forgetfulness the only abyss where he could be lost.

A threat, an immobility, against which my head rests, full of distress and pain, and what turns this into a kind of dizziness is that he doesn't seem more distant to me, but on the contrary, too tangibly present, as though the discomfort of forgetfulness were already drawing him to the surface. I turn in his direction with more difficulty, but with the exhausting feeling that he has never been so close and that if, in order to think of him, I were not obliged first to pass through the thought that I am forgetting him, I would hold him in a proximity that would pierce through all reserve. Thinking of him had always been a subterfuge for determining a place for him and distancing myself, for a moment, from that place, but at present I keep hesitating to summon him to where I am for fear of drawing him into a speech already obscured by forgetfulness. Because of this, I have to avoid him, keep on my guard, put him on his guard too, explain to him the danger our relations are putting him in, a danger all the more obsessive because I don't have a clear view of it, because he alone could help me understand it better, understand why he is exposed to it. What I sense is that this danger makes him closer, more tangible, attracts him, attracts him to me, which is where the danger comes from—and how could I imperil him? A thought that belongs to the threat, just as mysterious, just as threatening as it is, a thought which I have never had before, at least not about him, and which I'm not sure I'm still having, a rarefied thought in which it is hard for me to remain, even though everything in it seems to me illuminated with a new, blinding light. When I say he is close, he is only more present, with a presence that is too immediate, that makes him close to me without making me close to him, that distances me from him instead, by keeping me here where I am. It would certainly be a sign of uneasiness, of weakness, if, instead of staying at a distance, he began wandering around very close to appearances, as he has never been tempted to do in his respect for my reason and the calm of his certainty. He lacks something, clearly, but I am incapable of finding out what, incapable of supplying it, just barely capable of acknowledging, of watching over that approach, and of struggling to keep it from being expressed through signs. I can't say I'm lying in wait for him, or if I am it is in my memory, as though the greatest danger were in seeing him appear there. I'm not lying in wait for him, but the feeling that I attract him more than he attracts me—that through my mediation a power is exercised that is already taking him to the frontiers of this world—is in some sense the root of the word "forgetfulness," the source of the disturbance I can't control, for it is a disturbing feeling, it conceals within itself a temptation difficult to overcome, in which I ceaselessly risk showing myself to be strong against myself. It is tempting to attract the unknown to oneself, to want to bind it by a sovereign decision; it is tempting, when one has power over the distance, to stay inside the house, to summon it there and to continue, in that approach, to enjoy the calm and the familiarity of the house. But perhaps I had already summoned it, maybe it was too late: this was the presentiment that made my time a dead time in which it seemed to me I was fighting in vain against something that had already happened, even though, despite everything, I retained this certainty: I will not yield.

Perhaps I wouldn't have felt so assaulted by this change if I hadn't suddenly discovered—a revelation that became wedded to the day, after which there was no more day for me—that I not only was hearing him speak, but that now I could hear how difficult, how impossible it was for him to speak. An overwhelming impression. One moment, and I couldn't doubt it: it didn't speak, it didn't make any noise, and yet it would have liked to speak, it desperately aspired to speak, after infinite efforts it came to the threshold of speech only to collapse on it, perish there, putrefy there in a breath whose last vibration I just barely perceived. How could I endure it? I asked him quickly: "Did you just say something to me?" and he answered me no less promptly: "But didn't you just speak to me?"—which made me glimpse more than I would have liked. I tried, at least, not to show it to him, I couldn't put him directly in the presence of my thought, so I confessed only the easiest thing:

"All these times I have thought there were too many words between us."

"Between us?" He seemed to descend into this question,

but I saw clearly that for me this interval, in the form of a ditch no longer had its depth. Suddenly, he said in a feverish way:

"Yes, we must speak constantly, without stopping."

"Do you want that?"

"It must be! Now! Now!" He said this in a tone so piercing, so bestial, that I became disoriented and in turn nearly shouted:

"Don't talk that way—not now."

Immediately afterwards, near me, there was a quick noise of something falling, a dull falling noise, without depth.

"What happened?" I said in a low voice.

His curiosity was instantly aroused.

"Yes, what happened?"

"It was a noise of falling, as though someone had fallen at my feet, just as I finished speaking to you."

"You had just spoken?"

"I was just saying to you..."

But I didn't linger over that word, I didn't linger over it especially since the same incident that had led to it now took its place: yet not entirely the same, it was closer, it seemed able to cross the threshold, the silence lifted under the effort of which I sensed the gigantic pulsation, a cry, the madness of a cry within which everything would break, more than a cry, a word, but already this had collapsed, the cry had not been delivered, and I, too, had not been delivered from it.

This incident, by good fortune, took place shortly before nightfall. Only the night could contain, could stop the effect of the tear it had made. For a long time I examined the thought that, as long as I was speaking to him, he would find in what I said, however paltry it was, an appeasement that would then allow him to answer me from the depth of his reserve. It is true that the anomaly only seemed to occur when he tried to come to me without my knowing or without waiting for me to clear a path for him. I was not even sure of this, for there were still too few instances, and at least one, the last, appeared to be an exception. Yet I could not detach myself from my remark, it seemed striking to me, just as I had always been struck by that power of initiative he had, which he very rarely made use of and almost always in a lusterless way, but in spite of that, I retained an extraordinary memory of it: every time, I had been surprised, shaken—frightened? a little frightened, as though all of a sudden I had understood that instead of remaining riveted to the chain of words, a chain so long it allowed him to roam all spaces with the appearance of freedom, he kept breaking the chain, and even more, that there was no chain and that chance alone allowed him to emerge precisely where I was and nowhere else. When I talked to him, I felt the weight of the chain, it was tiring but reassuring, the chain was only a fiction, but the weight was real. When he appeared by way of roads that had not been prepared, everything seemed capable of happening, everything that had been acquired through days of effort and struggle seemed to be lost in order to make room for him: I didn't have the feeling of a true freedom, it was something else, I don't know what, a possibility that wasn't a possibility, a simplicity that overcame the imposture, but one from which nothing arose; it was a beginning, not even a beginning, perhaps not much of anything; when I summoned it up in memory, what I called initiative resembled one word too many, one that might have leaped over the series, but, after having distanced all the rest, made a place for itself there and strengthened the imposture. Perhaps, after all, nothing was more disappointing. All that remained was to understand why, within this disappointment, I wasn't disappointed, why, in this moment when I had to think of it as of a lost possibility, I found it so painful to have to renounce it, so distressing to commit myself, once and for all, to preventing him henceforth from coming unexpectedly and, in order to do that, always preparing the way for him, anticipating his initiatives, going before him, talking to him constantly, without stopping, without leaving any emptiness and without ever breaking the chain, so that he would not stray outside himself. A duty I did not want to shirk, but why this task? Why, in the calm of the night, did it appear to me, in the end, prodigiously difficult, but also prodigious, to the point of giving me back, at the moment when I was about to collapse, a superabundance of strength, an impetuousness of movement that didn't concern itself with anything? I understood it when I realized that this task had brought me back, without my knowing it and by an unsuspected path, to the word "write." In the circle of the night, this word suddenly rose up like a radiant intuition, as though it were presenting itself for the first time, with all the youthfulness of an indestructible dream, all the seriousness of a task I might not have the strength to bear, but that would bear me, on condition that for an instant I provide it with a point of support. I wasn't trying to recover all the reasons that had been pushing this word to the forefront for so long: everything, in that moment, was converging on it, everything was igniting in order to make it shine, and in its light the sovereign exaltation of the last day was already rising and setting.

As soon as the feeling that it was necessary brought me to my feet, the poverty of the day was what struck me, however, what made me feel, once again, how close to appearances my companion must be, how thin these appearances were. Yes, it was this that I saw first, the extraordinary thinness of the day, its tenuousness, its superficial brilliance. It was certainly a beautiful day, but terribly worn. I was standing at the table now. I was alone, with a different sort of solitude. I said to myself: "I must forget everything that happened before this night. I have a task to perform, and I also have the strength to perform it, the two fit each other exactly, as a cut fits the knife blade that made it. No doubt my strength is divided up, spread out through the whole of my life, whereas the task is concentrated in a single moment in which it waits, but it waits patiently; I can't fail it; with or without me, it will be accomplished." I was fully aware that what I called "my task" was astonishingly simple, that in truth it was already entirely realized, completed, there before me, and that now I had only to see this, make it apparent to my eyes. But for this, I would have had to relax for a moment, and I couldn't because I was paralyzed by the idea that my relations with my companion had lost all their simplicity. Never before had I spied on him. Never had he given me the feeling he was spying on me. Perhaps I was constantly occupied with him, but in this occupation I was free, all too free. I wasn't watching over him, I wasn't waiting for him, I talked to him and to talk to him required of me a very great effort, but this effort was made as though in my absence, in a spot where, nevertheless, I was so firmly gathered that I couldn't desire anything that wasn't immediately given to me. But now I found before me this thought that we were separated by forgetfulness, that within the forgetfulness he could be imperilled, that my duty consisted in preventing him from emerging from his depth, in pushing him back with my hand, the slightest pressure from which had once been enough to keep him at a distance, whereas now, it would surely require all my attention, all my strength, all my life, to preserve in one single point the integrity of the day. This made me nervous. I would have needed to be able to look at things calmly. Surely there were still more resources in them than I could suspect. I said to myself:

"Be patient with yourself; be alone for a moment; abandon everything, abandon even the night." But these words only agitated me, gave me a feeling of the emptiness that had to be filled up, the real words that I lacked in order to succeed in that, my desire to return precisely to the night in which I had approached them and, in my expectation of that night, I no longer saw anything of the day but its dreamy lightness, the light that seemed to have lost the edge of its manifestness and in which I could not make out anything, not even that the day was not lacking to me. Yet, the strange thing, in the corner where I was, near the table where, however, I wasn't writing—I couldn't call it writing—was that at no time did

I lose the instinct, the certainty, that here, at least, he would remain himself, that in this place, as he had promised me, a moment would come when "he would do everything for me." I kept remembering what he had said, and it was this memory I presented him with when I asked him:

"Don't you want to help me now?" I waited for his answer with a faith, a hope, that he must have sensed and that I sensed in turn when he said quietly, probably after quite some time:

"I can't help you. You know that—I can't do anything."

I was driven from my place by these words, it seemed; I had to go to another spot, another room, probably the kitchen where for a moment I found the tranquil light of summer again and looked at it with a shock of pleasure, but I didn't linger there, for I had the feeling time was pressing. Once I was back in the room, where the darkness of the day made me hesitate, I heard him ask me, with some anxiety:

"What did you just do?"

"Why, I drank a glass of water."

"Are you in pain?"

"I was tired, but I feel better already."

"Yes, it takes a moment to go away. Don't you want to rest?"

The truth was that I wanted to walk a little more. I felt a certain dizziness, a strangely solitary fear:

"We're completely alone."

"Yes, we're alone."

I walked, I took a few steps. Having become used to the darkness, I recognized the familiar space of the room, the tranquil openings of the large bay windows, a little closer to me the table, and almost next to me an uncovered and disordered bed.

"I think the best thing for me now would be to lie down."

"Yes, that's right." Almost immediately after, he asked me:

"You're tall, aren't you?"

But I didn't realize where these words were coming from, nor why they enveloped me once again with the impression of naturalness that had always marked our relations. I didn't realize it because I seemed to hear him in the tranquil simplicity of the past, but when I answered him: "Fairly tall," and he added: "Couldn't you describe to me what you're like?" I had such a strong feeling—probably at finding myself once again in the truth of his reserve, at the very moment when I feared I was left out of it—that I could only think of answering:

"Yes, that's easy." As I said this, I thought, in fact, that there was a mirror on the wall on the other side of the table, though I didn't intend to look at myself in it, but the memory of that mirror helped me say to him:

"I believe I look rather young."

"Young? Why?"

I thought for a moment:

"It's because I'm thin."

A remark that didn't seem to reach him, he seemed so occupied with allowing the word "young" to come to him, profoundly, in a disturbing way, repeating it as though he wanted henceforth to confine himself to it, to the point that, understanding that he wouldn't let go of it again of his own accord, I made haste, in order to deflect him from it, to find another reason: "And also because the face is very bright," which did, in fact, attract him strongly, while at the same time inducing him to raise this doubt, which he expressed shortly afterwards:

"But isn't there also something dark about it?"

I stood firm:

"No, it may be too naked, formed in too hasty a manner, but the eyes are bright, they have an astonishing brightness, in fact, a brightness that is cold, then suddenly brilliant, but most of the time very calm."

"How do you know that?"

"I think I've been told that."

But he pursued his advantage:

"Who told you that?"

"People."

"Ah yes, people. People"—a word that seemed to awaken an ominous echo in him, but he did not stop there. He went on:

"Extraordinarily calm?"

"Maybe not always."

"Maybe too calm!"—in a way that would have made me fear once again that I would never see him tear himself away from this word, if he had not abruptly ended by saying joyfully:

"Well, I see, I see," as though really, for him, something like a portrait had emerged from me.

Despite this joyous tone, I couldn't help thinking he wouldn't be satisfied with such an incomplete picture. I would have liked to make it more expressive, bring it close to the truth, which, through my fault, he had not correctly penetrated. I would especially have liked to go back to a trait that seemed essential to me, show him that this face was usually very gay, that this gaiety penetrated even the darkest moments, moments from which, even then, arose the glimmer of a brightness that was joyful, perhaps distant, almost absent, but all the more tangible because of that. I said to him:

"You know, there is a smile on that face."

This immediately pleased him in an extraordinary way; he asked feverishly:

"Where is it? In the eyes?"

"In the eyes, too, I think."

"Even when you're asleep?"

I thought about it: yes, even when I was asleep. While I was trying to imagine how he pictured that smile, he suddenly said to me, with that ferreting, unilluminated sort of eagerness he had:

"People like that, don't they?"

"Yes, they probably liked it." I almost asked him: "And do

you like it?" but I didn't do it, I didn't have time to decide
to do it, because he added: "I see, I see," and then I had the
feeling that this time he had really taken possession of this
face, that at least he was going to begin to carry it off toward
those regions where it eluded my power of attraction, regions close to which I would try to advance, without yielding, either, to the inclination that attracted me to him. I must
have spent a long time reflecting on what I called his sphere,
the abrupt lightening of our relations, a lightening which,
however, didn't seem to me to correspond to anything new,
as though I merely realized, now, that they had never really
changed. Then this idea occurred to me—that if our relations
were the same, it didn't mean he himself had remained iden-
tical; it seemed to me I should have asked him this: "Haven't
you changed a little?"—which I already heard him answering with: "But you've changed too!" and wouldn't that have
led me to say to him: "You mean you're not still the same?"—
a thought that was more like a shiver than a word, but even
though this thought was terrible to look at, I stared at it
anyway, I let myself descend into it as far as that point from
which I did not turn away, even when I had to hear something cry out that had neither form nor limit, something
revolting, the mud of the deepest places, the frenetic vitality
that did not bother either to recognize me or to let itself be
recognized. If I could succeed in doing this, it was because
this was still only the reflection of a thought. At least I didn't
refuse to do this until the moment when, being still within
the powerful meditation that enveloped me, I noticed that
my eyes were open on something that I didn't at first grasp,
a point, not a point, but a blossoming, a smile of the whole
of the space, which expressed, occupied all of the space, in
which I then recognized precisely what I had wanted to
describe to him, a smile that was free, without hindrance,
without a face, that radiated softly out from this absence,
illuminated it, gave it a resemblance, a name, a silent name.
I looked at this smile without surprise, without disturbing it,

without being disturbed by it, as though this calm had gradually been penetrated by the revelation that at this moment the figure was entering the sphere, that there it was being accepted in the form in which it had been described, that the smile now belonged to the distance, that I had really given it to the distance, that in this gift the distance would find nourishment and a temporary safeguard against forgetfulness, which had as a corollary this idea—that right now, in some way, I did not have this smile, this face.

How long this lasted I can't imagine, it wasn't an imaginary time, it also didn't belong to the time of things that happen. After the first contact, I began to look at him with more precautions; I must have been afraid that if I stared at him in too lively a way I would lose or destroy what I had so few guides for grasping. But I felt, on the contrary, how little this view depended on my gaze, how it eluded my gaze without remaining a stranger to it. This was not addressed to me, perhaps it came from me, I could still recall it, but as a picturesque detail, without importance: at present, it was the tranquil smile of no one, intended for no one, and near which one could not dwell near oneself, not an impersonal smile and perhaps not even a smile, the presence of the impersonal, acquiescence to its presence, the evasive, immense, and very close certainty that no one was there and that no one was smiling, which was, however, expressed by an infinite, fascinating smile, so tranquilly fascinating that when the uneasiness in the face of this fixed point returned, I could only look at it calmly, in the calm that radiated from it, and also in a friendly way, for an intimate ray of friendliness came to me from it. Nothing calmer than that, a visible circle of calm—and yet, something that immediately made me see something else, not so calm, a calm not soothed, shivering, as though it hadn't reached the point from which there is no longer any return, as though it wasn't free, yet, from all faces, still desired one, feared being separated from it: sometimes giving me the feeling of wandering desperately around the face, sometimes the hope of drawing near it, the certainty of recapturing it, of having recaptured it, an unforgettable impression of its unity with the face, even though the face itself remained invisible, a marvelous unity, sensed as a happiness, a piece of luck that dispersed shadows, that went beyond the day, something for which one was prepared to sacrifice everything, a thrilling resemblance, the thrill of the unique, the force of a desire that again and again recaptures what it once held—but what is happening? resemblance does not cease to be present behind everything, it even imposes itself, becomes more majestic, I divine it as I have never seen it, it is the moving reflection of all space, and the smile also affirms its immensity, affirms the majesty of this resemblance which is almost too vast, the smile seems to lose itself in the resemblance and through the smile the resemblance seems to become a resemblance that strays, without resemblance. A fissure still infinitesimal: the smile only smiles more mysteriously, as though the lost unity was even closer to the truth of this smile, which, nevertheless, slowly, with infinite patience, has already become once again the pain of an empty smile, the calm smiling of that pain. Oh, endless returns, vicissitudes of a dispiriting slowness! At certain moments, I can't doubt it: what is smiling really is the smile of a face, of a face I don't see but that remains the indestructible certainty of that smile. Then, once again, I can't doubt it, it is ineffably poised on emptiness; in it, the emptiness opens on a smiling allusion torn across by a slight derision.

How long has this lasted? The feeling that I'm the one involved in this must play its part in this absolutely slow movement, this unmoving oscillation, which I would out distance in vain, with which, on the contrary, I must unite even more through my own immobility, and once again it approaches what I believe I still know, it rises, it reveals a possibility of unique joy, which is perhaps no longer mine, but no matter, it is a joy for itself, a happiness in which I don't have to participate, which illuminates in me even the feeling of not being here in order to take part in it, and, once again, it unbinds the unity of that joy, it detaches it, detaches it from itself, as it has detached it from me, but with such patience that the smile of absolute distress always becomes, once again, the smile of absolute peace, and the latter, again, the reflection of the empty depth. Sometimes I say to myself: "Don't look at that, let it decide between you and him, let the decision leave you, don't go back." But the fact that this no longer depends on me creates a relationship I don't want to avoid. No doubt I have decided it, but to witness the solitary struggle of my decision, its tenacity, which, in the element of hunger and emptiness, makes it find satiety and fullness once again, to feel how it would need to be decided again and again to the point of exhaustion, and nevertheless, in its detachment, to perceive the point of truth that makes it smile—all this, too, belongs to the decision, and I must not free myself of it, nor allow myself to be distracted from it. No doubt I could still do it? Who would not liberate himself from the depth of a reflection? And yet it seems that already it has taken possession of the day, that it insinuates itself into it, fascinates it, alters it, becomes the work of another day. True, this does not spoil its beauty: it is also the smile of the day and this smile is only the more beautiful because of it, as though in this smile its protective envelope begins to dissolve and into this dissolution penetrates a light that is closer to me, more human. Perhaps everything that dies, even the day, comes close to man, asks of man the secret of dying. All this will not last very much longer. Already, I sense in a distant way that I no longer have the right to call out to my companion—and would he still hear me? where is he right now? perhaps very near here? perhaps he is right under my hand? perhaps he is the one my hand is slowly pushing away, distancing once again? No, don't distance him, don't push him away, draw him to you instead, lead him to you, clear the way for him, call him, call him softly by his name. By his name? but I mustn't call him, and at this moment I couldn't. You can't? at this moment? But it is the only moment, it is urgently necessary, you haven't said everything to him, the essential part is missing, the description must be completed, "It must be. Now! Now!" What have I forgotten? why doesn't everything disappear? why is it someone else who is entering the sphere? then, who is the one involved here? wasn't it I who took the drink? was it he? was it everyone? that wasn't possible, there was a misunderstanding, it had to be brought to an end. All the force of the day had to strain toward that end, rise toward it, and perhaps he answered immediately, but when the end came, after the scattering of a few seconds, everything had already disappeared, disappeared with the day.